Necropolis

Case Files of the Undead

Book One

Blue Deco Publishing
www.BlueDecoPublishing.com

Necropolis
Case Files of the Undead

Cover by Denise Lhamon & Colleen Nye
Editing by Jennifer Meltzer
Formatting by Colleen Nye

Published by: Blue Deco Publishing
PO BOX 94 Potterville, MI 48876
BlueDecoPublishing@gmail.com

Copyright © 2016 Blue Deco Publishing & James Silverstein
Printed in the United States of America

All rights reserved.

No part of this book may be reproduced or transmitted in any form or by any means, electronic or mechanical, including photocopying, recording or by any information storage and retrieval system, without written permission from the publisher.

The unauthorized reproduction or distribution of a copyrighted work is illegal. Criminal copyright infringement, including infringement without monetary gain, is investigated by the FBI and is punishable by fines and federal imprisonment.

This is a work of fiction. All characters and situations appearing in this work are fictitious. Any resemblance to real persons, living or dead, or personal situations is purely coincidental.

-To Dave.-

One less victory for the Lord of Shadows!

Stay tuned after the end for a sneak peek at:

Case Files of the Undead

Book One

The Case of the Scarlet Starlet

Episodes

Necropolis Episode 1
The Dead Giveaway
Pg – 1

Necropolis Episode 2
The Dead Rose
Pg – 59

Necropolis Episode 3
The Dead of the Night
Pg – 125

Necropolis Episode 1
The Dead Giveaway

They say that there's a calm before the storm. As usual, most of what 'they' say is dead wrong. A lot of things have to happen before storms come into being, and most of them are far from 'calm'. There's all sorts of atmospheric goings-on, dealing with temperature and pressure and humidity. But beyond all that, before a storm can start, something has to fall.

In this case, that something was a single button.

It fell from the top of the Andaris Building, tumbling and gaining speed, but when it hit the ground, it did so with little fanfare; just a click and a crack as it broke in two. No, while the button was the first thing to drop, it was hardly the main attraction.

"Huh. Looks like I lost a button."

Jack hung upside-down by his ankle as he made the observation, gently touching the edge of his jacket. The zombi's grip on his leg was like a vice as he dangled.

"Mister Foster, I would think you'd be more interested in the ... gravity of the situation."

The voice was like nails on a chalkboard, and the man it belonged to was only a few steps away on the roof.

"Sorry, Fritz," Jack spat back, "I don't take anything the Nazis say seriously. You've already lost. Like your corpse friend here, you just don't seem to know when you're *already dead."*

The necromancer sneered. "Perhaps the Fatherland just knew how to build us better. But that shouldn't be foremost on your mind, Jackie. The fact that you're dangling ten stories above an entire horde of hunger-enraged zombis would be, I think, a bit more important to you. Even if you survive the fall, they'll strip you to the bone!"

Jack squinted as he looked down. The entire sea of unhumanity moved like a mass of rotted flesh and evil hunger. He then looked back to the man from Berlin.

"All right, you have my attention."

"Good," the little man cackled. "Now, just tell me where the rubies are."

Jack smiled. "Go to blazes."

Before the Nazi could react, Jack kicked his henchman's hand, hard. There was a crack of breaking bone... and Jack plummeted downward!

To Be Continued!

"That was amazing!" I heard a kid in the lobby say. "He's dead for sure!"

"Nah!" His companion, a beanpole of a teen commented. "He'll catch onto a ledge or something! Jack's too clever by half for any of that!"

Their argument continued as they left the theater. I just

grumbled. Movies never got the details right. Zombis didn't go on hunger frenzies like that. The Andaris Building was only six floors. And it was obvious that the rubies were hidden inside the fake Bible at Jack's sweetheart's house. As much as I disliked the film, though, I so very much appreciated how easy it was to sneak into the air-conditioned theater.

The weather in Chicago had been stubbornly stuck on "broil" for almost three weeks, and the angry cloud layers above were taunting us mere mortals, as well as those not-so-mortal. To add to the heated matter, a firebug had been loose in the city, and the past four targets were all buildings in my run-down neighborhood. It meant the cops wouldn't be looking into it too deeply, and everyone was even further on edge.

It was the fifth anniversary of me coming back from the front, and I needed a damn drink. The Nazis were no picnic, but at least over there you knew who you were fighting, and when you shot 'em, they stayed dead. At least to begin with...

I'd been there when all that changed. When the Nazi occult experiments finally bore fruit and the dead began to walk again. It was too little, too late, the papers would say; we still won. We broke Hitler and his goons, even with their new nightmare army. But every anniversary my hands shook. Necromancy was too big a genie to put back into the bottle, and even with laws against it, the dead still walked.

Days like that day, I almost felt like one of them.

I stumbled from the theater to my tiny office like a man hung over, but it was far from the truth; I hadn't been able to afford a good shot of booze in almost two weeks. The staggering was more from the pain that a baseball bat swung like it was aiming for the outfield can do to a man's hip. All I can say about that is, you should've seen the other guy. He's doing six now for assault with a deadly, and none of that was due to the aforementioned baseball bat. Guess he's just lucky.

But this ain't about him or the case around him. This is about that fateful Tuesday in early September, and the first thing to drop before the storm.

I lumbered into the office and cursed as I almost slipped on another small pile of overdue bills near the mail slot. Crossing the room, I dropped into my chair and winced as the pain shot through my hip. Another day at the office, made even less fun as I was my own boss, so there'd be no playing of hooky without the head man finding out. I decided to ponder ways to remedy that situation while leaning back with my hat pulled over my eyes, as at that point I had nothing else on my plate outside of filling out the expense reports for the last job, an annoyingly straightforward divorce surveillance.

My brainstorming disguised as a nap was interrupted by a knock on the door. I stopped leaning back. It must've been a client; the landlord never knocked.

"Enter, and of your own free will," I beckoned.

The door opened slowly, and standing just outside was one of the biggest men I'd ever seen in my life. Not muscle, no; the prospective client was wide enough that, for a moment, I wondered if he'd even fit in the door. His entire frame showed a man who'd never met a meatloaf he didn't like.

His suit was impeccably tailored, and he held a hat in his hands that, I have to admit, was small enough that I expected it might look comical if properly perched atop his head. I restrained myself from any such observation, however.

"I said, come in." I repeated, "Or stay out, really. It's your day to waste."

That seemed to snap him out of the stare he was giving me. Gingerly, he stepped in and shut the door behind him.

"Marcus Sage?"

I nodded.

"The private investigator?"

"Unless my license got revoked, yes. Please, have a seat, Mister...?"

"Brown. William Brown. Thank you."

The thanks seemed sincere, but the big man seemed to have trouble deciding whether he actually wanted to sit.

"I'm afraid I can't offer much," I said, trying to make things a little more comfortable for the man. "I have some water... That's about it, really."

Brown finally sat. "No, that's okay, nothing for me."

He stared, studying me. I stared back, repaying the gesture. Finally, after a minute or so, I sighed and leaned back in my chair again. "Mister Brown, we've established who and what I am, and who you are. Perhaps we could move things along to what brings you here? We don't seem to be making progress beside that."

An embarrassed cough followed. "Yes, of course. Sorry about that. I just never... Look, I've got a problem. I've been to Cartier and Doonse. I don't think they can help me with what I want."

"Illegal?"

He looked horrified by the prospect. "Nothing of the sort."

"Please continue, then."

He collected himself again, squirming a bit on his chair. "I've had something stolen from me, Mister Sage. Something of import that... Not to be too indelicate... I don't expect the police to be able to get back to me in any reasonable amount of time."

"And the stolen item is...?"

Again, the pause. Again, staring at me, as if deciding whether this was in any way a good idea.

"A briefcase. Locked. It has in it confidential papers I'm not able to discuss."

I nodded and thought for a moment. "And you think it's being held by one of the undead."

He blanched and stammered for a moment. I waved it off.

"Pardon if I cut to the chase on this one. You've come to a private detective, though you've been to others. You've been to Cartier and Doonse and because you didn't tell me you balked at their price, I assume you've got the money to pay them. Thus, while I am cheaper, you're not looking for a bargain. You don't like the idea of trusting a black private investigator, as is pretty obvious by your constant uncomfortable stare. I'm only as trustworthy and as of good repute as half a dozen other agents in the city, so what does that leave? You've decided to go to the detective who has a small but serious reputation for dealing with problems of a necromantic nature, and one who has little problem doing jobs the cops don't seem to be interested in... Which means ones done in the Necropolis."

Brown once again looked a little embarrassed, and began to raise his massive frame from the chair opposite me. "Look, maybe I should go elsewhere..."

I motioned him to sit down again. "Don't worry, Mister Brown. My reputation is not unfounded. If the haystack is the Necropolis, I can find you any number of needles before the week is up."

The big man nodded, though he did not sit. His gaze turned away from me as he took a moment to wipe off his glasses. "And the cost?"

"Five dollars a day, plus expenses. They'll be itemized."

He seemed to consider it. "A good figure."

"And well worth it. Do we have an accord?"

Another pause, but this one was shorter than the others. I think I'd struck a little close to home with my assessment, and he didn't want me to think I had. He nodded, sat again, and reached across my desk to shake my hand. To his credit, he made it look natural.

"I believe we do, Mister Sage."

"Good. I'll type up a contract before you leave. But before that, perhaps you can tell me a bit about this briefcase."

****

The story came out quickly as I typed. Brown had been putting together some family documents to prove a piece of heir-ship to a family estate. The entire thing had been put in a locked briefcase, and his assistant, Ed Jones, had last been seen with the case two nights previous. Ed hadn't turned up for work the next day, and calls to his house had gotten nowhere. A cursory investigation and an interrogation of the neighbors by Mister Brown had found that Jones had taken a cab heading deep into the district in which I plied my trade. Brown had no idea where the final destination was, nor did he suspect that Jones knew anyone in the neighborhood. There had been no sign of Jones since.

The papers got signed, and a three-day retainer got handed over without any sort-of fuss. Usually at that point my clients would leave and let me get to work. This time, however...

"They said you were there at Dachau."

I nodded and leaned back in my chair, but didn't volunteer anything.

"What happened? I mean, what really happened?"

They always wanted the goddamn story.

"Not much to say," I started, trying to keep it brief. "We got there, and there were zombis. We held out as long as we could, and thankfully our request for reinforcements came expeditiously. Some of us died. We came back home."

"There were rumors..." He ventured, "A necromancer colonel."

I stared at him coldly. "I don't know. I was busy fighting for my life."

To his credit, Brown didn't look too sheepish at the retort. He frowned a little, and nodded.

"I understand, Mister Sage." He stood and said, "I should probably be going."

"You probably should," I agreed. "I'll call you

tomorrow if I find your briefcase."

"Thank you. Thank you very much."

He lumbered out the door, and as I leaned back in my chair, I couldn't help but think about the fact that as much as Mister Brown wanted his briefcase back, he certainly didn't seem to care whether I found Mister Jones at all.

****

46th and Maxwell was on the edge of the Necropolis. There was a nice swath of highway that separated it from the business district to the north, and right after the war, when the fear of the new ghetto was strong, fences had been put up to keep the good, clean citizens of the dirty city away from the rotting flesh on the south side. The wooden slats are still there, covered with the grafitti'd demarcations between the dead and those that hate them.

Huddled against the fence, however, was Wally Dugan's taxi dispatch. Wally had a mean streak a mile wide, and an egalitarian hate. he hated everyone equally, dead or alive. As I approached the garage, I could already hear him chewing out a driver.

"You call this a sheet?" Wally spat, his toupee barely staying on his rapidly-shaking head. "I've seen five-year-olds who can do math better than this!"

"Sorry, boss..." The young driver cringed.

"Yeah, I know you're sorry! Everybody's goddamn sorry these days! Now go redo it and get it right this time!"

He threw the paper to the ground, and the kid picked it up and scuttled back into the hot darkness of the bay his hack was in. Dugan turned his furious gaze to me, and spat.

"Kids today. Goddamn kids."

I nodded, and Wally walked with me into his office. His anger was still blazing hot, but it dialed down a couple of degrees as we sat at his desk.

"What is it this time, Sage?"

"Fare out of midtown. Two nights ago. Name was 'Ed Jones,' if that means anything. Was heading our way."

"Fer chrissake," Wally muttered. "Two nights ago? You think my drivers keep accurate logs?"

"How's Edna doing these days?"

It dropped his protest into grumbles. He turned and started looking through an unkempt file cabinet. "That crap ain't gonna hold up forever, Sage."

I merely shrugged. "I was only asking after her health."

He turned to face me again and slapped a file onto the table. "Night's receipts. And she's fine, thanks for asking."

He continued staring at me as I rifled through the file. Finally, he couldn't take it anymore, spitting it out. "And how's that bastard Rogers?"

I looked up from my work, as if Edna's ex-beau was the farthest thing from my mind, "Oh, he's still up on charges. Looks like the former Missus Rogers will be taking him for everything he's got. I doubt he'll be bothering Edna again."

It elicited a cold smile from Wally. "Good. No one messes with my sister's heart."

"As you say." I said, finally finding the right bit of paper. My look of disappointment made Wally's grin even wider.

"Where are ya headed?" he asked.

I sighed. "The Blackpoole."

Wally laughed, "Oh ho ho! Even big bad Marcus Sage pauses at the doors to hell. Good to know!"

I pushed the file back across the desk, then stood and tried not to wince at the pain as I walked out. Wally called out after me, "We're even now, Sage! Don't come back!"

****

It was late afternoon by the time I got to the south end of the Necropolis where stood the Blackpoole. The entire building sat like an obscene squatting steel-and-brick spider at the edge of a run-down park that never saw human traffic after the sun set. Adding to the overall cheerful ambiance was the fact that the city's firebug had torched his first building two doors down from the 'poole, and the residue of that horrific blaze had tarred the sidewalk and road outside of the club a greasy black.

There were two dead at the door, a zombi and a ghoul. The perfect pair, really; the zombi for the mindless strength, and the ghoul for actions that needed the conscious thought that zombis could no longer create.

Fred, the zombi, despite having a stick-figure body, looked as if he could bench-press a Packard. After working the Necropolis long enough, I'd learned to gauge that sort of thing. He was a product of the most basic of necromancy; a body that would follow orders, but never have complex thought.

Marvin, the ghoul, was dressed to the nines and held out an ashen hand to halt me as I stepped up. Like all of his kind, there had been more advanced, expensive necromancy performed to keep his mind intact after his demise. His voice was like poured oil, slick, but unpleasant to get on you.

"Club's closed, Sage."

"I'm not here to dance, Marvin. I'm here to see Mamu. You know she's always happy to see me."

The ghoul's facial expression was impossible to read, but he did pause for a moment, lowering his hand.

"Happy isn't the word I'd use, Mister Sage." I wasn't sure if he was joking with me or not. Even after all this time, it was still hard for me to tell with ghouls.

Marvin looked to the zombi, and whatever dark communication they had sent the unthinking dead scuttling back into the club.

I waited.

"Hot one today," I offered.

"They say it might storm." The same poured-oil voice. At least he was polite. I've known a lot of ghouls who just don't care about that anymore. Then again, Marvin was getting paid to be nice.

My thoughts on the matter ceased as Fred shuffled back to his place beside the door, and made a mechanical gesture for me to go inside. I raised an eyebrow. Fred always did seem almost thinking. I tipped my fedora, and walked past the ghoul into hell.

****

The front room of the Blackpoole was actually hotter during the day than the outside. Days like we'd been having, it was a practical oven. I shuddered to think what it would be like in the evening, but still, people came. Before the war, the place was strictly local; a good club for swing, and during the prohibition, a place you could get a drink without fear of John Law. After the dead had come knocking, the club had changed. Now the ghouls came here, and there was a steady stream of those brave souls who figured going to a hotter-than-hell club full of demon jazz, whiskey, and the walking dead was something of a fling. The brave at heart sometimes even came back for an encore.

Emil, the man behind the bar, was a ghoul. There are those that'll tell you they can tell a zombi from a ghoul on sight, but even with all the times I've worked with, for, and against 'em, even I have trouble. Sure, zombis tend to be a little thinner, a little more slack-jawed, but sometimes people die like that. There are zombis that can pass as ghouls, and though I can't imagine why they'd want to, ghouls that can pass for zombis. Hell, with enough self-care, there are even ghouls that can pass as living.

Emil gave me a nod as I passed. "Sage. Hot enough for you?"

The heat of the front room wasn't on my mind, though. I was soon in the back, and the back office was air-conditioned and sound-proof, all the things to put a person at ease after traveling through the purgatory-like front room of the 'poole. But I wasn't at ease. I was in the presence of Mamu Waldi.

"So nice to see you, Marcus. It's been far, far too long."

Mamu was pouring us both drinks from the small bar in her office. Even though it was early in the day, she was dressed for the evening to come; a long black dress with enough of a slit to show her legs to the knee. From there they went to forever, and I knew more than one poor Joe who came here just at the chance of seeing them. I can't say truthfully that I'd been immune to that lure myself.

But it wasn't her body, her dark hair and skin practically made of shadows and obviously designed by a particularly ingenious devil to tempt men out of their senses, that drew so many. It was her voice. Mamu's voice was like every half-dream you've woken up from and wished you were still asleep. It was honey and warmth and the purr of satisfaction that only comes from some pretty secretive places. She had the voice of an angel and a devil all in one, and she knew that quite well. Only the two zombi muscles in the room were likely immune to her charm, and I can only say "likely" on that account.

She smiled as she caught me staring, just a little bit. "Cat got your tongue? I can't be that distracting, can I?"

"We both know that's not true."

The smile upped a notch. "Spoilsport."

"It's the scotch," I lied. "I haven't had a shot in over a week."

She sauntered over to where I sat in the comfortable-but-not-too-comfortable chair on the client side of her desk, and handed me the glass. "Poor man has the shakes. Let me fix that for you."

Her fingers touched mine as the glass was passed, and it gave me a little shiver. Sadly, the shiver made my hip move, so it was all punctuated with a wince.

Mamu looked concerned. "Are you all right, Marcus?"

"It only hurts when I get hit with a baseball bat."

She chuckled, and sat on the edge of her desk, those legs swinging gently, hypnotically. "I heard."

"News travels fast," I grumbled, then shivered again as I downed the scotch.

She poured me another. "You know nothing gets past me, sugar."

I downed the second and nodded. "S'why I'm here. I'm looking for a briefcase."

She laughed as she stood and walked back to the other side of the desk. "I was hoping it was a social call. You don't come around much."

"I'll try to remedy that."

"You won't." She shrugged. "So what's in the briefcase, and why would I have it?"

"Confidential papers, and the guy who had it was here two nights ago. No idea where he is now."

She moved to the other side of the desk. This was business now. "Hmm. Let me think. Anything in particular special about the guy?"

"About five eight, five nine, red hair."

"Ah, yes. I think he went home with Nancy."

"And Nancy would be...?"

She smiled, with a little hint of wickedness. "A regular. She likes the living."

I grumbled; a detail my employer had left out.

"Dammit. Didn't take him for a Renfield."

I'd touched a nerve. She motioned for one of the zombis to come forward. He lit her cigarette. I raised an eyebrow; normally she'd let a little thing like that roll off her back. I went with the only thing I could think that had put her in a state like this.

"Slow business?"

Mamu rolled her eyes a little. "You don't know the half of it. Normally the place is jumpin' every night of the year. Last week or so, though..." She shook her head.

"It's the heat."

She laughed, but it was a harder sound. "Marcus, the heat never stopped anyone from wanting to have a little illicit fun. You of all people should know that."

"Maybe they've given up on the dead?"

"Don't think it's that, either. The people here... We get some pretty strange types. Maybe I've got competition elsewhere, but I haven't heard anything. You?"

"I'll keep an eye out," I lied. Renfields, by the numbers, just give me the creeps. I've done some snoop-and-snitches that ended up with those, but even though I can deal with the undead as people, I just don't like the thoughts that come to mind when I think of them getting horizontal with the living. Ghouls would be bad enough, but... zombis? I shuddered. Best to stick to the case.

"Just tell me where I can find this Nancy, and I'll be out of your hair."

"For a while at least, Marcus, I'm sure. No one walks away from here for good."

Before I could retort, she scribbled a note and pushed it

across the desk. "You owe me one now, shamus. And I always collect my debts."

I grabbed the address and she snapped her fingers. One of the zombis lifted me out of the chair by my collar, and a moment later I found myself sprawled outside the club in a dirty, soot-covered alley. I'd escaped hell reasonably intact. Mamu was right, though. I knew I'd be coming back eventually. No one really escapes hell.

****

No one really escapes hell. It was a lesson I figured I'd learned fast enough at Dachau. We were there for four days. The newsreels were never released for that mission, but everyone knows the tale, or thinks they know. The dead were coming back to life, and they wore the swastika.

From our entire unit, twelve of us made it out alive and intact. Four of the bodies were never found or accounted for. In the years since, half of the dozen have been locked away in nice quiet padded rooms where they can scream away their remaining years without offending anyone. Three took the quicker way out with noose, pistol, and rat poison. That leaves three of us, all in our quiet little struggle to get out of hell.

But some people don't try to escape their hell. Some people embrace it.

I wore out a good piece of shoe leather looking for Nancy. She had a spot right where the address said, mortuary row; close enough to the north-east edge of the Necropolis that the good clean people outside of it could possibly spit in your hair, if they cared enough to.

I'd gotten used to the stares in the army from those who didn't like my skin color. It still annoyed me that people who shared my particular pigmentation would give me the evil eye because I happened to be amongst the living, and they were decidedly not. To say the landlady gave me the cold shoulder was putting it mildly. Her house was full of good girls, she said. No male visitors, she said. No, she hadn't seen Nancy, and wasn't sure if she remembered where she might be or when she might come back. And then the door slammed in my face, with a half-heard litany about "coon" this and "Renfield" that retreating back down the hall.

So, I did what any good private eye would do. I broke in.

The fire stairs up the back led to a squalid little hall, and Nancy's room was the first on the left, according to the mailboxes. Neither the fire door nor hers gave me much of a problem.

Now, understand that the dead have their own scent. It does have a touch of decay in it, but almost all of them do their best to hide it with oils or what-have-you. That's why, when I opened the door and got a whiff that would gag a donkey, I realized that either Mister Jones had very low standards, or there was more dead than alive here.

Both Nancy and Ed were sprawled out on the kitchen floor. She had the back of her head caved in, the brain destroyed. The bookend that likely did it was lying beside her.

Ed was more of a mess. A pool of cool blood, and a slash from ear to ear. Professional job. I avoided the body and checked the bedroom. No briefcase. No briefcase anywhere. But there was one thing. Three glasses on the counter. There'd been a third person here for whom Nancy, or Ed, or both, felt comfortable enough to pour a drink. There was only lipstick on one of the glasses. Guest was most likely male.

I knelt by Ed's body and looked it over. Just under his sleeve I saw some sort of mark. Rolling up the cuff, I was rewarded with a bit of tattoo that looked something like a child's scrawl of two blackbirds and some kind of scribble between them.

I took out my notepad and a pencil and started sketching it. Just then one of the other women of the house walk past the open door. As I mentally cursed myself for leaving it ajar, she took a step backward, and locked eyes with me. I knew she was about to scream.

I quickly motioned her to keep silent, and, bless her heart, she did so, though she was trembling like a leaf.

"I know this is horrible," I said, stepping into the hall and closing the door behind me, "But I'm an investigator. I'm trying to figure out what happened here. Can you tell me if you saw anything?"

She shivered, her eyes still stuck on the door. "I... What happened to Nancy?"

"Someone was in there with her and her beau. Did you see anyone come in?"

She shook her head, then paused. "No, wait, they got a delivery from the drug store down the street."

"Happen to see who made the delivery?"

She shrugged. "Some kid. I... Is Nancy dead?"

I nodded. "Afraid so."

The woman collapsed, sobbing, into my arms. I held her for a moment, then my eyes trailed down the hall. The landlady had just come upstairs. "What the hell is going on here?"

I knew an exit cue when I heard one. I was out the back door, down the escape, and gone from mortuary row before you could say "wanted for questioning."

Later, when I found a payphone, I'd call the drugstore. Of course, they had no record of any delivery. They didn't even have a delivery boy. Hadn't in years.

****

That night I slept fitfully. Even before the war, dreams had never been my friend, and afterward? Well, I know what caused my comrades-in-arms to get locked away in mental hospitals. What they saw when awake, I only saw in dreams. I'm only marginally sure I got the better end of the deal.

In my mind I was back at Dachau, but this time there were no reinforcements to save us. The waves of the dead kept rising, with the maniac colonel in the back, screaming in German to rally his damned troops and whistling that eerie tune of his. I was disarmed. I was being dragged toward a building black as pitch. Smoke was billowing with a charnel scent, and I couldn't scream. I couldn't even breathe.

I shot awake as I fell out of bed, my hip singing symphonies of pain as I landed on it. I tried to call out in harmony, but I realized that I still couldn't scream. The nightmare was over all right, but I couldn't scream... I couldn't breathe!

It was like a hand crushing my throat, but there was

nothing there. I desperately tried to get myself upright, and stumbled toward the door, grabbing the metal wastebasket on the way. For once in my life, I was vaguely pleased that my apartment was so small.

Spots were beginning to form in my vision, and I stumbled against the door, almost falling backward again as I pulled it open. There was a brown paper package on my doorstep, and I didn't have to open it to know what it was.

For those of you who don't know what a Glory is, it's the severed hand of a zombi (or a ghoul, I guess) kept alive by necromancy rituals. When placed outside a person's door, it will slowly choke to death whomever is in the house. As it's a slow process, it's usually placed at night while everyone's asleep. If everyone in the house dies, the Glory decays instantly. Thought of as one of the more gruesome assassin's tools, it was one of the first things to get banned when the anti-necromancy laws got enacted. It's also a hell of a lot more difficult than you'd think to actually make one.

If you end up the victim of a Glory, the quickest way to stop the charm is to cut off the Glory itself from air. I slammed the metal wastebasket over the package, and thankfully it was as air-tight a seal as I'd hoped; my breath came back immediately, and I slumped heavily against the inverted can, gasping for breath.

What did it add up to? Someone wanted me dead. Someone powerful, with a whole lot of necromancy behind them.

It also meant I would have to go into the heart of the city, and talk to the only man in Chicago even bigger than the necromancers and the mob put together.

****

I disliked traveling downtown from the Necropolis, especially when I didn't have cab fare. The border areas between the neighborhoods were sketchy, and while I didn't mind the occasional stink-eye from those who lived near the edge, there was something about being from the southwest side that made people want to avoid you at best. At worst... I'd had enough back-alley beatings for being in the "wrong neighborhood." I didn't feel like re-living them.

I took a bus and sat in the back with a few others who kept their distance when they realized where I'd gotten on. Ironic. They were the ones who were talking about how we all needed to be treated equally. How we'd done our duty overseas, and how there was a level of human dignity at stake. I guess that dignity didn't extend south of 46th Street.

The ride was mercifully short, so I didn't have to inflict myself on those fine people for longer than they could stand me. I'll admit, I was already in a state when I got to my destination, and the party was just getting started.

The building that held the local offices of the Bureau of Necromantic Affairs used to be a big hotel right across from Grant Park, smack-dab in the center of downtown Chicago. Now it's all offices and security. Propaganda posters line the windows: "Keep Your Eyes Open!" "Protect Them From the Darkness!" "Dead Men Tell Tales!" and my own personal favorite, "Necromancy Breaks the Laws of Nature! Only Criminals Break the Law!"

Maybe I shouldn't have come in the front door. Maybe I shouldn't have been carrying a briefcase with a tightly-wrapped Glory in it. Maybe I should've backed down when the tall security guard intercepted me. Whole lot of maybes. None of them happened.

"Excuse me, sir." the guard said.

"No, excuse me." I tried to walk past him, but he shuffled into my path.

"This is an exclusive entrance."

Yeah, that's what I'd been pushing for. Something that would give me a nice hard rage. Being told to come in the back way because of the color of my skin? That was it.

I stopped and stared directly at the guard. "What's your name?"

He paused for a moment, unsure as to whether I was someone who could get him into trouble.

"Vickers, sir."

"Vickers? Get out of my way. I've got business with your boss."

"You'll have to go around back, mist--"

I decked him.

Other guards began to swarm, and I began flailing.

Despite what you might see in the pictures, numbers mean a lot in a fight. They wrestled me to the ground, and I think I might've had a chance to get out of it... But then the briefcase popped open and the Glory spilled out.

My last conscious memory was a collective cry of anger, and a boot coming down on my face.

****

I woke up in a holding cell somewhere underneath the BNA building. How long I'd been there, I had no idea. I stood and stretched, and tapped on the door. I didn't expect an answer, and didn't get one.

I sat for about an hour, letting my anger simmer, before the door opened. There, framed in the amber light of the hall, was the man whose pictures had been in the paper for months. A little on the short side, but muscular enough that you could tell it wouldn't be a good plan to get on his bad side. Blond hair starting to gray, in a cut you could set your watch to. The director of the Chicago branch office of the Bureau, and the man who'd personally saved my life more than once: Hollis Brody.

Brody had made his name after we both came home from Dachau as a fearless crusader against necromancy. He was there during the first raids against the Black Smugglers in '45; I'm sure you've seen the photo of him slapping the cuffs on Dark Roger. He did a whirlwind tour with the feds, snatching up those who were still offering pockets of resistance. He'd been a golden boy in the war, with two heroism medals for his work saving our bacon at Dachau, and now on the home front he was a golden boy again. His credentials weren't hurt by the fact that his twin brother, Nate, had been killed by the very necromancers Hollis railed against. There were rumors of a Senate run if he could get Chicago cleaned up. He'd taken two major necromancers off the playing field since the Fourth of July. Things were looking up for him.

At the moment, however, he was looking down. Down at me sitting on the floor of the cell.

"All right, Marcus, what the hell were you thinking?"

I felt like a child being scolded. Unfortunately, Hollis was in the right, and I did deserve it a little.

"I was thinking that I'd have to come up the back way and wait in line until they decided I was worthwhile. Then I'd have missed Christmas."

Hollis reached down and gave me a hand up, just as he'd done during the murderous days at Dachau. "You wouldn't have had to wait, Marcus. I've always got time. But you bring a Glory in here? I had to pull strings just to stop them from throwing you in federal prison!"

I was on my feet, and I took the fact that he was leading me out of the cells to be a good sign. Still, my anger wasn't burnt out yet.

"It seemed like the best way to get your attention."

He brushed off the thought. "Channels. You go through channels, we'll talk."

We got to the elevator, and while the operator gave a look that let me know that this was "exclusive" as well, Hollis' nod seemed to be as much pass as I needed.

"There were never channels in the war," I said.

"Yeah. War's over, Marcus. At least the war over there is. Everyone goes through channels now."

"I haven't got time for channels, Hollis," I said as the elevator door closed. I took the sketch of Jones' tattoo out of my pocket. "What's this?"

He stared at it, and took it from me. "Necromantic mark. German."

"It do anything?"

He nodded. "The folks that worked in some of the

bigger labs had 'em. We think it was basic precautions, like wearing safety goggles in a lab."

The elevator stopped on the first floor, and Hollis ushered me out. It was then I realized that he was maneuvering me towards the front door.

"Hold on, you're not even concerned about this? Or where I got a Glory? Goddammit, Hollis!"

Hollis's eyes went hard. The comrade-in-arms shtick was up. "Marcus, at the moment I'm up to my fucking eyeballs in investigations that make a Glory and a tattoo look like cheap Halloween decorations. I haven't got time to fix the problems in the Necropolis. But understand one thing. One day, the BNA's eyes will turn in that direction. When it happens, you don't want to be remembered as the guy that had to be put in a holding cell because he socked a guard and brought ILLEGAL NECROMANTIC MATERIAL into the Bureau's offices. Do I make myself completely fucking clear?"

The last words were practically spit at me. I had the sudden urge to do something that would get me sent right back to the holding cells, but I held it in check. He'd saved my life. Twice. I owed him this at least.

"Clear as glass," I said. I looked towards the door out to the street, then back to Hollis. "Don't suppose I'll get that sketch back."

"Don't suppose you will. Go home, Marcus. Deal with whatever corpse-carver has got you in his sights. When it's over, I'll buy you lunch. Up here."

Hollis just couldn't get his hands dirty. That was the long and short of it. Not if he was shooting for office like everyone thought he was. At that point, even brushing gently against the Necropolis left a sooty stain not easily removed. It was all for the best that, on my way out, we didn't shake hands.

****

I knew that taking the bus would just make me angrier, so I walked the four miles back to the Necropolis, stopping only to grab a hot dog. The fact that my budget could barely afford it didn't help my mood any.

By the time I hit 43rd Street, however, my cares about the gastronomic hit to my wallet vanished. I saw smoke rising from the Necropolis. It was possible it was just someone burning trash, but when you've had an active arsonist in the neighborhood...

The smoke was coming from my apartment building. I ran like hell and kicked in the flimsy back door. I started yelling into the darkness, but there was no response.

As I stepped in, I could see the flames licking against the front half of the building. The fire was still starting, but it was too big for me to put out. I yelled again. No response. I half-hoped that the four other people who lived here might've been out somewhere.

I was about to turn and get the hell out of there when I heard a groan from upstairs.

"Crap."

I vaulted up the stairs three at a time. The fire was actually worse towards the top, and the metal bannister left a nice scorch on my left palm. I was already choking on smoke. Whoever was here, we both had to get out fast.

I winced as I turned from the stairs and looked down

the second-floor corridor. There, at the far end, was a man struggling against a teenage kid. The man looked well-fed and strong, and it only took me a moment to realize why he had to struggle at all against the stick-thin teenager he was confronting. He was fighting a zombi.

"You stupid goddamn mindless piece of firebug crap!" the big man said, trying to grapple further with the undead.

"Get out of here!" I yelled, moving forward to break up the fight.

The big man turned and saw me, and he gave an almighty shove to the zombi, throwing her into a patch of flame on the wall. The zombi's desiccated corpse started going up like tinder, making an odd little whistling and furiously steaming, while the big man turned his attention to me. His beefy right hand swung, but I ducked and answered with a right cross that knocked him back on his heels a bit.

"This isn't any of your business!" he grumbled, then raised his fists again.

"Someone burns down buildings in my neighborhood? I make it my business!"

He swung again, and I blocked it, trying to get a jab in at his face. His other hand slammed up into my gut, doubling me over a little bit. He headbutted me, and I fell to my knees. I grasped onto the hem of his jacket and swung feebly as he raised his fist for another blow.

There was a mark of two blackbirds and a squiggle on his wrist.

"Where the hell did you get--"

His fist came down, the lights went dark.

****

I woke up coughing, but breathing. People two doors down had done the smart thing when they saw the smoke and called the fire department. Say what you want about public service in Chicago, but we get real serious when it looks like a fire might spread. The firemen had found me upstairs, along with the charred remains of a teenaged zombi. Missus Abernathy had also been found, unconscious from smoke inhalation, but she was now breathing steadily. The Billings family were away on a weekend vacation. Oakley was probably still at work. Thank the lord for small favors; beyond the zombi, no casualties.

Already, the news was out, though; arson by the undead. By morning, I was sure the story would be in the papers, and those living in the Necropolis would find whole new reasons to be looked at with fear, scorn, and hatred.

I didn't have a home to live in now, so I went back to my office and sat heavily in my chair. The mark. A necromantic precaution. On Jones' body, and now on the guy who seemed to be... Wanting to stop a zombi from burning down my building? The whole idea made my head swim. Brody was going to be no help in the information department, and my limited knowledge of the facts behind necromancy was taking me nowhere fast. It wasn't about the briefcase anymore. This was bigger, I was now sure of it, and someone wanted me off the case really, really badly. I had no choice. I'd have to go to the one person I knew who would talk to me and who knew the necromantic underworld like the back of her hand.

I'd have to go back to hell.

****

The Blackpoole was jumping that night. They'd gotten a swing band out of New York that had been headlining all over the east coast. There was a line out the door. Luckily, it was the same two monkeys at the door as before. Marvin waved me forward and gave me a knowing nod. "The mistress isn't available right now."

"Mind if I go in and wait?"

He shook his head. "You're welcome here, Mister Sage."

"That's sort of what I'm afraid of."

The humor of the unliving is a tricky thing, but I think I made him grin a little.

I heard the groans and protests of those still waiting in the sweltering night as they saw me cut in front and move inside. Almost immediately it was drowned out by the sound of the band. They were loud, the horns cutting through the smoke and crowd inside like a hot knife through butter. The beat was almost infectious; despite my pain and exhaustion, I found myself tapping my foot to it.

I walked to the bar and ordered a drink. Figured it was better to ask for forgiveness than permission when it came to a tab, and as I'd been seen in Mamu's company, the bartender acquiesced without comment. Soon, some of the city's finest whiskey was coursing through my body, reminding the little aches and pains that there was still comfort in the world.

The crowd looked to be half-and-half tonight, dead and

alive. It's actually harder than you might think to catch a ghoul at a glance if they've spent a decent amount of time and effort to look like the living. Zombis are a lost cause, but those that went through the process that kept their minds intact after their animation could, and did, take steps not to be confused with their mindless brethren.

Necrophilia was a term that got thrown around in stuffy circles, but the name on the street, the name that you'd not say in front of the children, was Renfield. Those that preferred the social and romantic attention of the dead. All sorts of crude jokes were passed about it. I could understand there was a lid for every pot in the world, but I just couldn't get a handle on that one. Mamu had once told me not to knock it until I tried it. I ignored her advice and continued to knock it.

It was after the band's third song that one of the house ghouls came over and let me know that Mamu had a moment if I wanted it. I followed him to a table in the corner. Mamu sat with two men, both dressed more expensively than anything I could afford if I saved up for an entire year. Even from a distance it was plain she was casually flirting with them both. As I approached, she took a long draw from her ebony cigarette holder and let the smoke drift out. "Gentlemen, this is Marcus Sage, hero of Dachau and private investigator."

The two looked vaguely impressed by the introduction. I thought maybe I should get business cards printed. I gave them both a courteous nod.

"If I'm not wrong, and I so rarely am," Mamu purred, "He needs my help on a very important case. I don't want to delay him. You boys can find something to keep you both busy for a few minutes, can't you?"

The two swells nodded, and one kissed her hand before

getting up and leaving. She looked after them with a fading smile.

"Not interrupting anything, am I?"

She patted the seat next to her, "No, of course not. They're lovely boys who've come all the way from Evanston to the big bad city. Their daddy owns... some company or other... and they want me to be the scandal they can brag to their friends about."

"Shocking," I falsely demurred.

"What's a girl to do?" She shrugged, making her black-and-gold dress do interesting geometry.

"You'll shoulder on, I'm sure." I sipped the drink I'd brought with me. "Oh, hope you don't mind. I'm running a tab."

"Of course not," she said, grinning, "I'll take it out in payment eventually, I'm sure. So, what is it that brings you back to my little corner of the world? I can't imagine it's just little old me..."

"As much as I'd like to say it is, I need help."

"Again."

"Again." I admitted, "You're savvy on what goes on with the necromancers."

She rolled her dark eyes. "No idea what you're talking about, Marcus. Necromancy is illegal. You know that. I don't touch anything illegal..." She paused, and took another drag from her cigarette. "But if I did... What would it be that I could tell you?"

I laid out what had happened with the arson, and what I'd seen on Jones' body.

"Tsk," she shook her head. "Poor Nancy. I told her fast living would be the second death of her. Another second-chancer that no one's going to mourn but me."

"So you've got no idea who the other guy might've been that offed her?"

"Sorry, Marcus. She went in and out with a lot of men. I can chat with some of the regulars if you like."

"Couldn't hurt. And the blackbirds?"

"The Krayenfusa."

I blinked. "What?"

She laughed, "Oh Sage, I thought you already knew or I'd have said something. It's a mark I've seen on a few men in here over the past month or so. I asked about it once, and got the name. I think it means crows' feet in German. Nothing else, though. I thought it was just something stylish."

The hairs on the back of my neck stood up. "Any of those guys here tonight?"

She cast a long gaze out on the crowd. "Hm... No, no... Oh wait! Yes, that one over there, dancing with Nikki."

My eyes followed hers. A big man, looked like the hired muscle type or I'm not the hero of Dachau. He was dancing inelegantly, but he didn't seem to care.

"Want him brought over here?" Mamu asked.

"No, no. You know his name?"

"Brian? I think. It's sometimes hard to keep track. Brian Mitchel? Maybe? Something like that. Starts with an 'M,' the last name."

I nodded. "You going to have a problem with me tailing him when he leaves?"

She touched my hand, and it gave me a slight shiver. "Darling, what you do when you're outside of my place is completely your business. Just don't cause a fuss when you're nearby, okay?"

I agreed, and for the next few songs, I sat with Mamu and watched Mister M like a hawk. The two from Evanston came back over and, after they realized I was no longer paying any attention to them or to Mamu, they picked back up on their flirting. I finished my drink, and waited.

****

Trailing Mister M was simpler than I'd imagined it'd be. He didn't have a car, which meant he was local, and he'd be walking. I'd done so many snoop-and-snitch jobs before, this was like a cake walk. He seemed blissfully unaware of my presence as we walked through the darkened streets of the Necropolis.

He turned east on Gower and started moving into the warehouse district. When the building he turned into seemed to have a password at the door (judging from his pause there when he knocked), I ducked to the other side and found some convenient crates to climb upon.

Peering through a skylight, I could see that the warehouse was divided into two parts. The first part looked like a small barracks. Mister M was getting set to get some shut-eye on a bunk, and there were at least twelve other guys in there. The place looked like it'd been inhabited for a month or two, tops.

The second part of the warehouse was in darkness. It was bricked off with cinder block, and had a tin roof over it. I had no idea what the heck they were hiding in a building-within-a-building, but I knew the answers to this crazy puzzle had to be there.

After a moment or two of indecision, my prayers were answered. A truck was pulling up to the back of the warehouse, right where the walled-off area was. I managed to drop down quietly onto the truck, and watched as two men came out of the front of the cab to open the warehouse doors.

It took my eyes a moment to adjust to the darkness. Then my jaw dropped.

I stared in disbelief. It was a pen of zombis. Not just a small handful of them, either. Dozens, maybe into the hundreds. They were chained hand and foot, and they each mulled a little bit in the small area that their leashes could reach.

Each one was dressed identically to the one who'd burned down my home, and none of them looked to be, in life, older than fifteen.

The drivers were on their way back, and I scrambled back atop the truck. They had long sharp prods that they were using to drive the dead onto the back of the truck, and they secured them inside once they were there. After closing the doors to the warehouse, they pulled out. I hung on tight and shuddered. There were plenty of zombis in the Necropolis, but this many that no one would miss? No. These weren't kidnappees, this was something different. Someone was making new zombis... But why so many? And why in a warehouse? The days of zombis as shock-troops was gone with the war. It was so damn expensive and time-consuming to bring someone back from the dead, people only did it if they were rich and or desperate. A warehouse of them meant so much in the line of resources... And what were they being used for?

****

I held onto the truck as it pulled out into the sweltering night. Under me, I could hear the low groans of the zombis, no doubt confused as to where they were going or what was happening. We were heading south, and doing so quickly.

We passed outside the city limits and kept driving into the night. I began to hope that wherever these guys were going, it wouldn't be too much farther; the sunlight would be a dead giveaway for me being on the roof, not to mention the outward peril of a multi-day journey, if that's what it was to be.

The truck started to slow about a half-hour later, and I breathed a sigh of relief. The overcast night was still pitch black, and I couldn't see a damn thing ahead until the headlights illuminated a rural house with a barn nearby. The house was dimly lit, and I was surprised to see maybe six or eight cars parked in the field nearby. All high-end, too; stuff that no one from the Necropolis would be able to afford.

The truck did a several-point turn, then backed up toward the barn. I slipped off during the automotive dance, and thankfully was close enough to duck behind one of the cars when someone with a flashlight came out of the house. One of the drivers came out to meet him, and I strained my ears to overhear the conversation.

"Twenty this time."

"I'm sorry it had to be such a rush. Twenty should last us a while. I've told everyone we can't be rushing things like this."

"Not my problem. So long as you--"

I missed the next few words. Sounded like the driver was talking about payment to someone named Paul? I didn't know.

The other man from the truck was "herding" the zombis into the barn. He kept two out, both girls. One looked about fifteen, the other about ten. I began to get a sick feeling in the pit of my stomach.

More conversation followed that I couldn't hear at all, and soon the drivers were headed back to the truck. I made a beeline for the back door of the house, and, as it was unlocked, quickly darted in.

The place reeked of alcohol and the dead. I almost gagged. Luckily, the back half of the house was pretty dark; I was relatively sure I wasn't going to be spotted.

I heard sounds from the floor above. Groans and muffled cries. The front door opened, and I heard the flashlight man talking quietly. "Now, come on upstairs. Everything will be fine."

I waited ten seconds, and, heart in my mouth, I followed.

****

Flashlight guided the fifteen-year-old to the end of a long hall, and I waited until they both passed through a door on the other end before I stepped up. A board creaked under my feet and I froze, but it wasn't for long. The noises, soft, horrible groans, from behind the other doors that lined the hall made enough background camouflage that no one would hear me.

I walked quickly and quietly. I suppose I already knew what I was about to find, or at the very least, I suspected it. Doors were ajar, and the groaning of the zombis was mixed with the noises made by men and women who had paid the price of admission.

Don't get me wrong; I *get* Renfields, even though I'm not one. I understand that love can come in many forms in this world.

But this? This wasn't loveplay, or even raw lust. This wasn't even the weirdness that working girls are sometimes asked to perform. I saw through an open door a zombi with her limbs twisted far beyond the breaking point for a living human, the man atop her biting her flesh. She groaned softly. Another door had a whole parcel of men going to work on one lone undead girl. From the look of things, they may've been at it for hours.

My gorge started to rise a little. This was sickness poured out onto the dead who wouldn't be missed, and whose bodies would last longer than any human stamina would allow. Zombis couldn't be hurt, not really. They couldn't say no, either. They were the perfect targets for the fantasies of the depraved.

I was almost to the final door when I heard the creak of the boards behind me. I spun, reaching for my pistol, but stopped as I saw the portly, sweat-stained man with bloodshot, drunken eyes leering at me a little.

"Spook! C'mere. This one's fun!"

He motioned me over, and, despite the blood rushing in

my ears, I followed.

The man opened a door, and within the room, like the others, was a bed and a zombi. This zombi, however, was a boy. He looked fresh. Fourteen, maybe. He stood, blank-eyed and naked, by the door.

I almost took a moment to try to figure out whether he'd been exhumed or if he was some recent murder victim when I noticed it wasn't only males in the room.

Lying on the bed was a girl. She looked sixteen. She was in her underwear. She was alive. She looked terrified.

The leering man chuckled. "See, now, honey? I've got either a big darkie for you or a zombi. Or it'll be me. One way or another, you're not walking out here without a little action tonight."

I belted the guy. Hard. He crumpled to the floor.

Before I could say anything to the girl, I heard other doors opening.

****

I got outside and vomited. Repeatedly. I knew I'd been heard, and I was trying to make like I was a guest. I hoped the darkness outside would make people not care to come after me.

Sadly, I was wrong.

"Hey! Hey you!"

I turned and my eyes went wide. It was that same huge son-of-a-bitch who'd been in my apartment building when it burned.

Recognition clicked in for him just when it did for me, and he charged at me. I'd learned his game from last time, though, and I came up with an uppercut, hard and fast, right into his chin. He reeled backward, and I closed in, trying to make the reach he had on me unimportant.

His strength was still immense, though. He pushed me off him and, although I ducked his left cross, his right hand grabbed my lapel and threw me to the ground.

I dodged his stomp, rolling to the side and getting to my feet, and flung a handful of dry dirt at his eyes. He raised his hands to block, and I got in two or three good shots to his rock-hard midsection. He dropped his hands and I gave him everything I had in three fast jabs to the nose. The third one finally staggered him back again, and he toppled back, his head smacking into the fender of one of the cars.

He wasn't out, but he wasn't going to be dancing the two-step any time soon. I dragged him back to his feet and shook him hard. "Where did you get the crows' feet? Who gave it to you? Where are they making the zombis?"

He groaned. "They'll kill me!"

"Them later or me now!"

He whimpered, "Look! Look okay! It's in the Hal Settler Building!"

"Who killed Jones? Where's the briefcase?"

He boggled for a moment, then laughed, "That's what this is all about? Jesus, that was all Pau--"

BLAM!

The gunshot made me roll back with a start. One of the other house guards had heard the scuffle, and shot at me.

The darkness, however, had made my sparring partner the new owner of that bullet. I swore under my breath and danced back amongst the shadows as another shot rang out, and another. I heard commotion coming from the house, and I started to run.

"Hold it right there, coon!"

Another shot, and this one closer. The guy was on the chase. I banked right. I only had one hope here if I wanted to stop him from shooting at me: I needed to make him worry about a different target.

The barn doors were already creaking as I ran to them. A shot slammed into the wall just to the side of my head; I could almost feel the heat from it. I could hear the guy quickly reloading. I grabbed the door and heaved!

The wave of zombis panicked by the gunfire and commotion knocked me to the side and started charging into the night. I heard the gunman curse, and shrieks of panic and dismay came from the front porch of the house. Another shot came my way, I think it hit one of the dead. I ran, yanked open the door of one of the cars and quickly hot-wired my way into gear. One more shot, and more shrieks, and I was out on the open road, speeding toward Chicago.

What the hell had I gotten myself into? A zombi slave ring? Mass-production undead? Some sort of Nazi conspiracy? I was in over my head, that was for sure... And at that point, as I sped off into the night, I didn't even know who I could tell.

****

As I got back into the city, a healthy dose of paranoia caught up with me. I couldn't go back to the office. If they knew where I lived, they certainly knew where I worked. I had no idea who these guys were, or what their end-game was, but after seeing what they were willing to do at the farmhouse, I knew my life wouldn't be worth a nickel to them.

I pulled the stolen car into a lot on Brower, and walked four blocks to an all-night diner. There, over a cold meatloaf special and a steaming cup of coffee, I began to think, and the more I thought, the angrier I got. Kid zombis. Slave kid zombis.

Just before the sun rose, I think the coffee jump-started my system. I was through with being the hunted, through with being chased and being scared. I was going to put an end to this, one way or another.

A block away was a payphone. I counted out a few nickels, and made my first call. It rang six times before a bleary voice answered.

"Hello?"

"Mister Brown, this is Marcus Sage, the private eye you hired."

The voice was suddenly a little more awake. "Have you found the briefcase?"

"No, not yet, but I have some leads I need to follow up on. Tell me, do you know someone named Paul? Pauls? Something like that?"

There was a momentary pause as, I figured, Brown was still waking up. "Pauls? Yes. Why?"

"It's a name I got attached to the theft of the briefcase. Mind telling me who that is?"

"Ralph," I could hear Brown coming up to speed, "Ralph Pauls. He was a friend of Ed's. You think he has the briefcase?"

"I think if he doesn't, he knows who does. Do you know where Mister Pauls might be?"

"He lives up on the north side, near the lake... I'm sorry. I don't know better than that. Is that enough to find him?"

"It should be," I said. "I should have the case for you by tomorrow, or at least news thereof."

"Thank you, Mister Sage. This means a lot to me."

"It's what I'm getting paid for. I've got one or two other stops to make first, then I'll head north."

"Excellent. A good day to you, Mister Sage."

"And one to you as well."

I hung up and made another call, then jogged back to my office. I skulked to the back of the building and felt like a rank amateur peeping in my own window. Thankfully, no one was waiting there for me. I'd hate to be shot while looking as much of a greenhorn as I was acting.

The stop in the office was brief. My pistol. Two extra clips. Pen and ink and a short note jotted down with Ralph Pauls' details and a brief explanation to whoever came in as to what happened if I didn't make it back. I took one last look over the place, shut off the light, and headed out into the early dawn streets.

The Hal Settler Building was in the warehouse district, not too far from where the zombis were being held. Made sense, I suppose, to keep the operations close together.. It had taken me some time to get there, and the ember of my rage had been stoked to a white-hot flame. There would be killing. Of that I had no doubt. I suppose the one good thing about living where I did was that I knew the police would turn a blind eye if a criminal ended up dead. I was counting on that.

Two men were casually smoking in the entrance way. I had one chance at this, and I hoped the pistol hidden in my pocket wouldn't be necessary just yet. They both came to greater attention as I approached, and one started reaching for something in his jacket.

"Whoa! Hold on!" I said, holding my hands up. "I'm just new."

I let my left sleeve roll down. There, plain as day, was the two crows of the Krayenfusa. The ink had only barely smudged on the way here, and I hoped the goons weren't going to look too closely at it.

My gamble paid off. The guards were only looking for the mark, they didn't care what color skin it was placed on. They waved me past, and I walked with all the confidence I could muster. The next room in was just an open space with a freight elevator. I guess my act as 'new guy' worked okay, as one of the goons shouted to me, "Third floor."

****

When the freight door opened up, I almost winced. The place looked like a set from some B horror movie. Wires and tubes and those "bzzzt" things were everywhere, and occult symbols were painted on the floor. Symbols I'd not seen since Dachau.

I moved in as quietly as I could; the hum of the machinery masked my sound for the most part. I crept in closer. I heard voices at the far side of the room, but I couldn't make out what they were saying.

It would be a straight shot to the speakers, over a patch of ground that had no cover. I was mulling it over in my head, and began considering how to make a distraction. The pistol slid into my hand, and I began figuring what looked like it might shatter the most easily.

Suddenly, a noise like a footfall to my right had me spinning around and leveling my gun. My breath eased and I lowered the weapon as I saw a boy there. He couldn't have been more than thirteen, and he was living dead. His eyes had gone wide, and I held up the pistol to let him know I wasn't going to shoot.

"It's okay," I whispered. "I'm here to shut this place down. Are there more of you here?"

He struggled. Asking complex questions to zombis was a recipe for disaster, so I shook my head. "More guards? People with these?" I motioned to my gun. Again, he struggled, then nodded slowly.

"This many?" I held up four fingers, estimating what might cause a problem for me. He shook his head. "More?" Again, the head shake. Finally, a stroke of luck. "Less?" A nod.

Three fingers, then two. Finally, the nod. Two guards. They might even be the ones talking to each other. I gave the kid a smile. "This'll all be over soon. I called the law before I came here. Just get somewhere safe."

The kid nodded and disappeared back into the shadows. Two guards would make it easy. Still, I didn't want to give up my advantage of surprise. I pressed my back to the wall and wedged myself behind a gently vibrating machine. For a moment, my shirt caught on a bolt, and while I tried to wriggle free, my gun clanked against the metal hide of the machine.

I froze. The conversation across the room stopped. I held my breath and tried desperately to struggle out from behind the machine. My shirt ripped, but I made it. Just then, the conversation started again. They hadn't heard me.

I breathed a sigh of relief. I was getting in close now. I could hear two people talking.

"It's all being taken care of. All of it. Don't worry."

"But I have to talk to him. Right now."

The second voice once again froze me in my tracks. It was Brown. Why in the hell was he here?

"He's busy. He'll call you when he's not."

"I'm afraid I insist!"

I heard the sound of a punch impacting a round stomach, and Brown gasping for air. It was time for answers.

I stepped out from behind the machine, gun drawn. "All right. Hands off my client. Get your--"

There were eight guards. All armed.

Brown was on his knees, gasping for breath. He looked vaguely amused as he peered up at me. I tried to figure out which way to jump, and whether there was any way I could save Brown. If nothing else, he owed me big time. I kept my gun level.

"First one that goes for their weapon gets a bullet in the brain." I said. "I don't care if you're alive or not. I know how to put you down."

A sharp pain and a crack. That's what you get when a monkey wrench connects with the back of your skull. Everything went sideways, and I fell to the floor. As I started to lose consciousness, I saw that damn kid standing behind me, grinning like the cat that got the canary, the blunt instrument of my downfall in his hands.

"Why...?" I choked out.

"Ah," I could hear Brown say. "I see you've met my son, Paul."

****

It couldn't have been that much later when my eyes opened again. There was blood down the front of my face, and everything was still spinning gently. I was tied to a chair, the rope biting into my wrists. A swinging light bulb above me let me know I was still at the "lab." Next to me, also bound, was Mister Brown. He looked in better shape than me. Two thugs stood over us. One of them smacked me across the face, I think just for spite.

I spat out a wad of blood, but I wasn't going to give the goon any more satisfaction than that.

"Brown, what the hell is going on here?"

"It's..." He wouldn't meet my gaze. "It's hard to explain."

"Can I make a guess? That briefcase you hired me to find, it wasn't personal papers, was it?"

A laugh came from the darkness, and its owner, Paul Brown, followed. He still had the wrench in his hand, and a wicked grin, like a kid who likes to pull the wings off of flies.

"Personal papers? Is that what you told him, father?"

"Paul, listen!" Brown said. "This is for your own good!"

Brown's plea was cut off by a left-cross from one of the goons. Paul tsk'd.

"I'll decide what's for my own good, Dad. Hey, shamus, you know what he thinks he can do? Bring the dead back to life."

"You seem to be living proof of that."

Again, the laugh. "Oh no, not that. Not ghouls and zombis. He thinks he can bring the animated back to real life. Heartbeat, growing old, and all."

I tried to keep the room from spinning by angling my head. All it served to do was to make it spin in the opposite direction. "So your dad's a little crazy. No one can do that. Why all the fuss?"

"Tell him, Paul."

Brown's moment of courage toward his son got him another smack from the goons and a hurt, accusing expression from Paul. Then Paul snapped his fingers, and one of the goons came back with a stack of papers.

"Dad got these out of Dachau, didn't you Dad? Oh, they're not the originals. But Brown was Braun once, and my uncle, Colonel Braun, was one of the minds at Dachau, wasn't he?"

I growled as I strained at my ropes. "That's why you asked? You didn't want to know the story at all. You just wanted to see if I saw the family resemblance!"

Paul's eyes went wide. "You were at Dachau? Oh this is too rich! Looks like the family secret almost came to bite you, father!"

I kept tugging. The ropes were tight, but if I could just get even a single knot untied...

"It will work, Paul! I swear it! I just need more time and subjects to experiment on!"

My blood froze. "That's what this was all about, wasn't it? All the child zombis? They were just practice?"

Paul practically cackled and clapped his hands happily. "Yes! Yes!" He then took a step towards his father and poked him in the prodigious belly with the wrench. "Why would I ever want to be alive, father? Do you realize what a better place I'm in right now? I live forever!"

"And as long as he didn't finish the experiments, he'd provide you with a line of playmates indefinitely."

"Playmates that are very profitable, shamus."

"Arson for hire?" I cast out a line.

Another cackle. "No, no that was... Well, let's just say some of the early experiments had a predilection for setting fires. Still not sure why. One of them got away from us, but I understand you took care of that one.

"There are other ways for the dead to be profitable, though. Perhaps I'll send you to a place where you can find that out first-hand!"

"The farmhouse?"

Paul's smile vanished.

"Yeah, I know all about that. Paid them a little visit last night. Can't say what's left of it."

The boy's eyes narrowed, and he snapped at another subservient. "Go check. NOW."

Paul was within two feet of me, and if I'd just gotten one single knot untied, I could've grabbed him. As it was, he swung the wrench down with enough force that I felt something in my shoulder give.

"I ought to kill you right now, shamus. But you're fun to play with. Let me tell you a little something. My associates tell me you drew a little crows' feet on your arm. It didn't look like very good work, I'm afraid. Everyone here has the real thing except you. Even father." He rolled up his sleeve and showed me the twin ravens on his wrist. "I have his expertise to thank for that. Do you know what staying amongst these symbols and machinery will do to a man without a Krayenfusa even for only an hour or two? They'll start to lose muscle control at first, then they'll start hearing whispers. There were asylums full of shrieking, half-paralyzed men in Berlin because of this. You were unconscious for almost ten minutes, shamus. You should start feeling the effect any time now."

"You sick bastard," I spat. "All this because you're Peter Pan and you won't grow up?"

"My father made me into this after I died from influenza. Why would I ever want to be anything else?"

"Fever rotted your brain, I guess."

It earned me another belt with the wrench, and I was seeing stars.

"This isn't like the pictures, shamus. I know you called the police. They're not coming. I own the police in this part of town. With the profits and the blackmail from the farmhouse? I own damn near everything. Except you. And no one's going to miss you."

"That's not what your mother told me."

He sneered, and simply tapped my knee with the wrench. "Flippant to the end. I think I'll enjoy watching you go mad."

I launched my head forward, and cracked viciously into his nose. He felt it, and reeled back as I stood, one arm coming loose from the chair. I couldn't get the other knot undone, but it was just as well; I blocked the wrench with the chair, and knocked the tool from his hands. Then I brought the chair down on his head.

Paul fell to the floor, stunned and howling, and his goons came for me. The two that were in the room reached out, and I kicked one in the knee, hard. I couldn't avoid the left hook, and it rattled my jaw, but this wasn't about winning. Now this was just about survival.

I tried to backpedal, but the second goon grabbed the leg of the chair that was still attached to my arm and yanked me forward. I went with the momentum and tried to bowl him over, but we both ended up on the floor. The first goon now had my ankle, and I kicked savagely with the other leg. I could feel his wrist snap beneath my heel as he yelped and fell back.

The goon on the ground with me put his hands around my throat and started to squeeze. I grabbed two of his fingers and yanked them backward as hard as I could. One of the snapped. I was on my feet again.

But Paul had warned me. I was starting to slow down. Whatever necromantic effect the crows' feet protected the others from, it was starting to seep into my bones. On the upside, it numbed me a little to the blow to the gut one of the thugs hit me with. The downside was that I was getting sluggish, and my swings no longer had the speed or power to fight off both thugs. To add to it, Paul was back on his feet with wrench in hand and a murderous gleam in his eyes. I managed to duck the first blow, but the second one had me seeing stars again. I kicked Paul once more and knocked him back a foot or two, but the goons had me, and I was soon pinned to the ground, the chair finally off my wrist.

"No more banter," Paul muttered. It sounded like I might've damaged his jaw a little. At least I had that.

"Shoot him now. We'll use the body for parts. Hope you have fun at the farm, shamus."

The thug whose wrist I smashed pulled out a gun. No, not just *a* gun; my gun. That was really the icing on this already-rotten cake. He grinned as he realized I'd noticed, and tipped his hat at his own cleverness. He pointed it at my chest and clicked back the hammer...

BLAM!

****

So that's what death is like, I thought. Not so bad, really. Didn't feel a thing.

It's amazing what'll go through your head when your life gets saved, and when necromancy is messing with your sanity.

****

All hell broke loose as gunfire filled the air. I tried to roll behind something. Anything. And I found myself face-to-face with Paul behind one of the metal cabinets. He was disarmed, and furious.

I laughed. "You dumb son of a bitch. I never said I called the cops. I called the law."

For as much as Brody and I were often at odds, at the mention of the possibility of a zombi children slave ring, he dropped what he was doing and sent an armed squad to take the place out.

Paul reached for me, but I grabbed his arms. He had the strength of the dead on his side, but I wasn't about to make this easy for him.

From the sound of things, his goons were putting up quite a fight. I kicked Paul off of me and rolled across the floor. For a moment, I made for Brown. Despite all that had happened, he was the client, and I needed to get him out of the crossfire.

Suddenly Paul was on my back, choking me. We were both at Brown's feet, and I hoped the fat man had the decency in him to choose me over his murderous, double-dealing son.

The choice wasn't to be made. Paul and I both saw at the same time. Sometime in the gunfight, Mister Brown, or Braun, or whomever he was had gained a ragged, bloody hole right above his heart.

Paul went berserk.

Thankfully, it wasn't on me. He started shrieking at the agents as he stood, screaming that he would kill whoever killed his father.

It took seven bullets, three to the head, before he went down. After that, the goons folded, and the BNA agents started passing around the handcuffs. I had the good decency to fall unconscious.

****

The hospital was cool, despite the temperature breaking 100 outside. I'd been in and out of consciousness for two days, but had finally managed to get myself upright without too much pain. There was a guard on the door, and when I was talkative, it was only an hour later that Hollis was there to take my statement.

"That's three you owe me," Hollis commented while taking notes.

"Two. The trip back to Rouen I could've taken care of myself."

"Eh, who's counting?"

"Then it's two. So... It's all over now, right? You'll send men to the farmhouse?"

"It'll get dealt with."

I didn't trust his tone. "And the papers?"

"What papers?"

I narrowed my eyes. "Goddammit Hollis! The notes Braun had. Or Paul. Or whoever had them. The necromancy notes from Dachau!"

Hollis shrugged. "Couldn't say. You know the place went up after you dropped."

"What?"

"Whole building burned down. Shame, really. But you know... Zombi arsonists..."

I struggled to sit up all the way. "That's crap and you know it, Hollis! I told you, it was part of Braun's experiments!"

Hollis stood and closed his notebook. "I don't know, big guy. I think that necromancer hit you a little too hard. Your memory's messed up. There were no papers. Just an illegal necromancy outfit preying on runaways. Good thing the Bureau got to it before anything worse happened."

"You son of a bitch!"

"Get some rest, Sage. Getting this excited can't be good for your health."

He clicked the light off as he left.

****

So that's the way it all went down. Sometimes the job goes that way. Answers to questions you never asked, and a mess of lies where you know the truth. You come up bruised and broken, and you never get the girl. All I had to show for it was a pay envelope for three days' work, anonymously slipped under my office door. I was too tired to even care where it came from.

Chicago continued to get unseasonably hotter as the next few days passed and I recuperated. I honestly figured that, so long as I kept my mouth shut, I might've escaped the worst of the whole messy business.

But the city has a funny way of paying back those who do either incredible good or incredible bad. The farmhouse thing... People knew it wasn't just an arson, and after a day or two, my name got connected. I had my picture in the paper. "Hero of Dachau Stops Necromancer's Slave Ring." An alderman even toasted me, though, of course, I wasn't present to see it. People were more than willing to use my name and my deeds for their own good, and while it normally would've rankled me, it brought me in a few new clients, so it all came out in the wash, as far as I saw it.

One night later that week, when I was a little tipsy from the glasses lifted to me at a local bar for my heroism, I walked up to my office door and the hairs on the back of my neck stood on end.

I really should've started paying attention to those. I walked in and immediately regretted it. Someone had broken in. Someone looking for little old me.

I felt the sap on the back of my head, and the room spun sideways. I'd be damned if I'd let it go at that. I spun, and noticed the guy must've practically leaped up to get me. Short guy. Short guy with my fist in his face immediately afterward, and him cussing and spitting blood as he staggered back.

But short guy wasn't alone. I turned in time to see a fist occlude my entire field of vision as a punch like a kiss from a Mack truck had me seeing stars, then falling into darkness.

"Bring him along," I heard as everything faded out around me.

It looked like it was true. No one really escaped hell.

Necropolis Episode 2
The Dead Rose

My eye opened. My left one. My right was swollen shut, and I couldn't move my arms. I had no idea where I was.

It took me a moment to put things together. I'd been in my office. I'd come in after a celebratory drink over the unexpected breaking of a case. Everything was looking up.

Then the roof caved in.

Well, it'd felt like it. I'd taken a blow to the head, and while I'd managed to put a fist into the face of the man who'd tried to take me down, his partner smashed my jaw with a fist like a zombi's. I'd started to black out, but I hadn't done it soon enough; a boot came down and turned out all the lights. Now I was tied to a chair.

"Good morning, Mister Sage."

I couldn't see who was talking, but the sound was coming from over my right shoulder. I grunted in response, "My wake-up call was for ten."

Sometimes my mouth gets me into trouble. Another blow to the side of my head almost put the lights out again.

Everything spun as a man built like a steam locomotive strode into my view. He must've been almost seven feet tall, and every inch was muscle. From the look of his face he'd taken a few hits over the years. I blinked, and realized that the room around me was a boxing gym.

"Statler's." I grunted.

"Still as observant as ever, Mister Sage."

The voice was still coming from my right.

"And it is that observational quality that brings you here today."

"I charge five bucks a day."

I got a shot that rocked my head forward, and I spit out some blood before adding, "Plus expenses."

"Witty to the end, I see."

"So this is the end?"

"That largely depends on you, Mister Sage. You have something I want. Mr. Williams here wants it as well."

The huge man cracked his knuckles.

"Mister Williams can't ask for himself?" I asked.

"Talking isn't his strong suit."

"So I gathered. Who is doing the talking, if I may ask?"

"My apologies, Mister Sage."

A diminutive man walked into my field of view. He couldn't have been more than five feet even. His stare, however, dared me to say something about it, so he'd have an excuse to sic Williams on me. After it was clear I wouldn't, he nodded politely.

"Buchanan," he said, "Chris Buchanan. Although many people know me simply as 'sir.'"

I searched my foggy memory. "Buchanan who runs the bookmaking on the south edge."

He smiled. "My fame precedes me. Yes, that Buchanan. And if you know that, you know that I'm a man accustomed to getting what I want."

"If you want me to call you 'sir,' you're going to have a really long wait."

Another blow followed. "Mister Williams doesn't like it when people disrespect me, Mister. Sage."

"I suspect there's a lot of things Mister. Williams doesn't like. A good left hook is one of them."

There was a moment's pause before the smash that time. I'd hit it right. Buchanan tsk'd, "You follow the fights."

"I saw the Williams and Brennan fight."

Buchanan held up a hand. "Are you trying to rile him, Sage? I can't imagine that would do either of us any good."

I shrugged. "It passes the time."

"You could do that by telling me what I want to know."

"If there was something in the office you wanted, you'd have already gotten it. If you just wanted to knock me off a case, you would've said so instead of dragging me here. I'm without a caseload at the moment, outside of a lost dog... You're not looking for Scraps, are you?"

"Very clever. I've heard that about you."

"So enough with the theatrics. Tell me what you want to know, I'll decide if I spit in your eye over it, and then I'll pick up where Brennan left off with Williams."

Buchanan looked uncomfortable. He'd bitten off more than he could chew in the banter department, and he knew it. I'd have to thank Aunt Agatha for that thesaurus last

Christmas.

"All right, Sage. You want it straight, here it is. You worked a job about two weeks ago. Peeper work. I want the photos."

I blinked. "Seriously? You want dirty photos I took in the Liston case? I'll admit, she's a looker, but I never thought the mob had to go that far for that sort-of thing."

"The pictures, Sage. They weren't in your file cabinet."

Either I'd come in while they were searching, or the men were idiots. Then again, the two were not mutually exclusive.

"Fine."

The two men paused. Buchanan sounded disappointed. "Really?"

"They're dirty pictures, and the case is already over. It's not something I'm willing to take a huge beating over, so let's get this over with. Take me back to my office, and I'll get them for you."

Buchanan smiled. "See, Mister. Williams? He can be reasonable. Untie him. Just understand, Sage, that any 'funny stuff' will see you back here for an extended sparring session with Mister Williams. Or..." He opened his jacket to reveal a shoulder holster with a nice .45 in it.

"Don't worry," I said, "You've got me dead to rights. I'll be good."

****

When we reached my office, I was lead out of the car, Buchanan keeping a close watch. His gun had gone back into the holster, but he'd made it clear that it could come out again to play with little or no provocation. I wanted to point out that it didn't make a lot of sense, shooting me would cause a ruckus and then he'd never get the photos he wanted, but the time for talk was over; Buchanan and Williams were amateurs, and I'd seen too many capers go south because of jumpy amateurs suddenly losing their cool. I just wanted this over with. I prayed there was no client waiting for me, and the way my work schedule had been going, it seemed likely.

My office had been ransacked. My file cabinet was open. The papers on my desk were scattered like autumn leaves all over the office. Even my trashcan had been booted across the room. Of course, I'd expected this; my playmates had already been here.

What I hadn't expected was a corpse just inside the door. I almost tripped on it.

"Did you leave this behind? Sloppy."

Buchanan and Williams were just behind me, and while they'd known of the destruction inside the office, they hadn't seen what was blocking the door. Buchanan shoved me forward. "Keep moving."

I managed not to trip on the body. Buchanan wasn't so lucky. He stumbled and fell to one knee.

"What the hell?" It was the first time I'd heard Williams speak. It wasn't a complete sentence, but I gave him marks for putting together a phrase.

"Not one of yours, then?" I asked.

Buchanan had risen to his feet, and looked down at the

corpse. His tone of voice told me, plain as day, that this wasn't at all what he'd expected.

"We can't take the rap for this!"

Williams nodded. "We goin'?"

"You're damn right!"

Buchanan spun around and tried to belt me with the gun, but I was too fast and caught his wrist. He glared at me, teeth clenched. "We'll be back for the photos. You mention this to anyone, you're dead!"

"Get the hell out of my office," I growled, and released his hand. Buchanan stepped backwards over the body, and pointed the gun my way again as Williams beat it down the hall. "We'll be back, tough guy. And next time it's gonna be you face-down if you don't give us what we want."

Some people say I have an over-developed sense of justice. Really, I just don't like getting pushed around. Any way you slice it, at that moment I felt the anger rising up, and I wasn't going to let these thugs think I was some helpless kid. My revolver was in my top desk drawer. I'd originally planned on getting the pair to get me to it, then working my way out of their clutches when I got it. Instead, I grabbed the pistol and gave chase.

Buchanan and Williams had run to the end of the block and were piling into their car. I wanted to put a bullet into their retreating vehicle, just to give them something to think about, but as I crossed the street, a brand-new Ford barreled down on me. I would've been smashed like an egg if a guy who'd been walking opposite me hadn't leaped out and knocked me aside.

I couldn't respond to his indignant warning. I wasn't even paying attention to the goons anymore. I had caught a glimpse of a person in the car speeding off. I had seen a ghost.

****

Let me tell you a story.

Once, back when zombis were fictional, before Germany decided most of Europe belonged to its goose-stepping leader, there was a boy who didn't know where he was going. Once there were pool-halls, and drunken benders, and even a stint in a juvenile facility.

Once, there was a girl. Ellen. She showed the boy there were better things in life. She showed him how to dream.

There was a dream of a house once. And a fence. And children. But all of those dreams got put on hold because there was a war, and the horrors at Dachau. But the young man kept going, secure that his dream was still there.

There was no Dear John letter. There was no news. There was an empty apartment and a landlady who said she just didn't know. The girl was gone.

It didn't take long for the boy's dream to unravel. He started drinking again. He tried to fix other people's problems because he couldn't fix his own. The dreams faded, and he got stronger as they hurt less and less.

But they never went away for good.

And now, the girl had returned.

****

I stumbled back to my office, stepped over the body, and sat on the corner of my desk. What the hell had happened here?

There was nothing for it. I put in a call to the police and started looking for clues.

I gave the corpse a once-over. Late twenties, fit. Blood was still warm. Looked like a couple of stab wounds.

His pockets yielded a drivers license so obviously fake that I didn't bother checking the picture to the man. There was also a .38 revolver in a shoulder holster. Whoever had killed him had gotten the drop on him fast enough that he didn't have time to draw. It would've taken a lot of speed or strength or both to do something like that if this guy had any experience with the gun.

I filed that away as sirens approached. Shame when they hurry for someone who's not going to get any better.

****

The Liston case had been shockingly straightforward. Infidelity work usually is, and I've had plenty of practice with it.

Howard Liston was the most long-winded person I'd ever met. The man had been sitting in the office chair across from me for an hour, and I'd learned only the first half of his life story. His family was from Massachusetts, he'd grown up the youngest of three siblings. He was currently in accounting. At that point I knew what he liked for breakfast (poached egg, toast). What I did not know, and this was the bit that bothered me, was what exactly he had been doing in my office.

"--- Now, if we talk about my sister's kids"

I held up a hand. "Mister. Liston, as intriguing as this all is, perhaps we could speed things up a bit?"

"I'm not sure what you mean, Mister Sage."

"It's almost noon, at which point I plan on going to the diner for lunch. Before then, I'd like to write you a contract."

His stared blankly.

"And in order to do that, I need to know what it is you want from me."

"Oh!" Liston looked embarrassed. "Sorry. I know I carry on."

"Nothing of the sort," I lied. "I'm just eager to know what it is a private eye can do for you."

"That... is a bit of a story. Six years ago I married Adelaide Whitfield. A fine woman. I'm sure you know how it is. Love and trust, and you think it'll last forever."

"You think she's stepping out on you."

He looked aghast. "Nothing of the sort!"

Okay, I'd jumped the gun. Still, if you'd been listening to Liston blathering on and on for the better part of an hour, you'd be anxious to get things moving as well.

"I apologize. Please," I ground my teeth. "Continue."

"Thank you, and apology accepted. No, I was married to Adelaide for two years. She died of a heart attack on our second anniversary. We were in Cuba at the time. She loved it there. Had to transport the body back. Such a mess. There was a scare over the possibility of some native voodoo being transported back."

"It was in the news. I remember."

"And it took almost four days to get her body cleared for the flight. In that time, however... I found out some things I wish I hadn't."

He paused, unsure how to continue.

"What things?" I offered.

"She was having an affair. With a business rival. She might've been giving him information as well. Needless to say... I felt a little violated."

"A natural reaction."

"Indeed. It took me months to get over it. Then Mary showed up. Mary Stevens. She worked in the same building my offices were in, and... There was a bit of a whirlwind. She made me feel alive again. Safe. In ways a man shouldn't need to be reminded of. She became my world."

"A lucky recovery."

"To be sure, sir. And... in some haste... she and I became engaged. Four weeks ago."

"Congratulations."

"Thank you." He paused. I took the moment to venture my guess.

"You're not sure you can trust her."

He looked at the floor, suddenly a shell of his former self. "No. I'm not sure."

"You want me to follow her, see if she's on the up-and-up."

He nodded.

I hated work like this. Still, beggars couldn't be choosers. I'd moved into a new place recently, and the bills were piling up.

"I get five dollars a day, plus expenses."

"That's perfectly reasonable."

His quick reply let me know he just wanted to get this done. I decided to oblige him. "I'll type up a contract, and we'll both have time to get to lunch."

****

I spent the afternoon at the cop shop, answering questions. No, I didn't know the guy. Yes, I had an alibi. Sadly, they didn't believe the later, and went so far as to tell me that Buchanan didn't do kidnappings. My swollen face tried to refute the fact, but they were having none of it.

Still, they couldn't link me directly to the murder. They cut me loose with a warning not to leave town. Like I had somewhere else to go when there was a mystery like this to be solved. And make no mistake; I knew I was going to solve it long before Chicago's Finest got off their collective behinds to figure out why there was one more non-moving corpse in the Necropolis.

****

Heading back, I was on autopilot. The blood on the floor would need to be mopped. I'd managed to snag a bucket and mop from the janitor's closet; I didn't want to give the janitor more to gossip about.

"Waiber" (according to his fake license) had been in my office looking for something when he was interrupted. As there was nothing of mine on the corpse, I could only assume whatever it was either was still here, or his assailant had it.

After cleaning up the blood, I stacked things back into the file cabinet. Buchanan and Williams had been looking for the Liston case photos, and had checked the "I – L" drawer. A good guess, but wrong. Neither did they find what they were looking for in "A – D", even though there were quite a few files labeled "divorce."

No, in order to find Liston's file, the boys would've had to look down in the "U – Z" drawer. Within was a big file marked simply "Unpaid." Liston's unwillingness to settle his bills had kept his pictures safe.

The sun was starting to set as I finished my once-over of the place. One would hardly know someone had been brutally murdered there. I triple-checked the lock on the way out, and with the Liston photos tucked under my arm, I made my way southeast. Once I passed Gower, I was in the warehouse district.

The buildings were starting that early stage of abandoned dilapidation that made them only slightly dangerous. "No Trespassing" signs were still generally obeyed outside of birds and rodentia. It had been two years previous, during a particularly heated divorce job involving a local alderman and not one, not two, but three exotic dancers... that I'd take up a tiny corner of the Mendelson warehouse as a hidden drop-space for sensitive materials.

I pulled the rusty-hinged door open and found the little space behind some of the steam-pipes. I could have the pictures if I needed them. If my office got a visitor who was smarter or more thorough than Williams, Buchanan, Waiber, or whoever did Waiber in, they'd get nothing and like it.

After re-locking the warehouse, I decided my next step was to pay Liston a visit.

****

The streetlights had just come on as I walked past the building I used to live in. It was still a wreck. Not just arson, but arson by a zombi. At least, that's how everyone heard it. Even here, in the Necropolis, that had turned a lot of evil eyes onto the undead. The zombis didn't care, of course; they still had no thought processes, and harassing them was like harassing a statue... A statue that, if sufficiently angered, could rip your arms off. The ghouls, on the other hand, were now even greater targets of scorn. Living in the ghetto of the dead was hard enough, but with every eye watching you, every tongue whispering that maybe you'd be the next one to snap and start burning buildings... I couldn't imagine the strain.

To make matters worse, the Bureau of Necromantic Affairs was starting to take an interest in my little corner of the city. In the past week, there had been three raids dealing with "unlawful necromantic activity," a blanket term that could've meant just about anything.

I'd tried to come out with my part of the whole sordid story, that the zombi in question had been part of a trafficking ring. The press carried my story, but after a while I realized that the fact that I was admitting it was a zombi was all that people heard, so I stopped talking. Last thing I needed was more chaos in the Necropolis.

I caught a cab to Liston's neighborhood. With most people inside having dinner, those that remained on the stoops to avoid the stifling heat were almost all children. I was being watched like a hawk by the darling little urchins. A black man had just come into their neighborhood.

When I knocked on Liston's door, one of the kids, more brave and curious than the rest, wandered over to interrogate me.

"Hey mister, what're you doing?"

"Looking for Mister. Liston," I said. "This his house?"

The child nodded, her pigtails bobbing.

"You seen him lately?"

Again, the nod, combined with a little "I-know-something-you-don't-know" grin. I sighed and forced a smile. "And when did you see him?"

"Day before yesterday. I don't think he's coming back."

I knew the answer before I even asked. "Why's that?"

"They took him away with a sheet over him. He's dead-dead."

I sighed. It looked like one of the many involved players had come here before trying their luck at my office. It also looked like Liston's bill would be permanently outstanding.

****

I caught a bus back to my little apartment in the Necro; no cab in Liston's neighborhood would've picked someone like me up. On the ride, I thanked whatever powers there were that I'd not said anything about Liston or the photos to the cops. If they thought they could link Liston's death to me, I'd still be there in interrogation.

From the bus, it was only a couple of blocks walk to my place. My neighbor, Barney, was out on his stoop. Barney was one of the few people in the city who always seemed to keep an eye out for other people.

"Hey, Sage! Welcome home!"

I tipped my hat. "Hey Barney. Hot one."

"Don't you know it! It's almost November, for gosh sake. You look like you've been through the ringer."

"Corpse in my office."

He chuckled and nodded. "He have a good case for ya?"

I decided not to disabuse Barney of the notion that I had a ghoul client. "Yeah. He has me looking for stolen rubies."

"Ooh, nice!" Barney grinned, knowing the joke for what it was. Thankfully, he didn't push it further. "So, I've got a chicken in the oven..."

"Barney, what would you do if I hadn't shown up?"

He shrugged. "Feed some to the neighborhood cats?"

"You're offering me food you were just going to give to strays?"

His smile broadened. "I'm still giving it to a stray."

I couldn't help but grin back. "Touché. Chicken it is."

****

Barney and I spent the rest of the night with chicken, television, and better beer than I'd expected. He asked me about what was really going on. "*After all, Sage, you're a celebrity now. Everyone wants to know about your cases.*" I humored him and told him I figured the next step in figuring out why the photos were so damn important was to talk to the other end of the case. After all, Liston wasn't going to be telling me anything more.

****

The next day it only took a few hours to get the goods on Liston's death. It would've gone faster if the people in his neighborhood looked at me more as "investigator" and less as "what the hell is the black man doing in our neighborhood?" I swear, if I die under mysterious circumstances, I don't care if the guy looking into it is a Martian. I expect those near and dear to me to cooperate 100 per cent until the guilty party is found.

But enough of that soap box. A few hours in, and I knew that Liston was as straight with me as he could be. The former marriage ending in Cuba, the romance with the girl from his office. Yes, Mary, that was her name. Seemed like a nice woman. Mary's description matched the photos I'd taken. Yes, Howard doted on her. Yes, he seemed shaken up over the past couple of days. But shot in his own home? Such things defy logic. He's in a better place now.

I'd never considered the medical examiner's office "a better place," but I kept my mouth shut.

Liston, it turned out, worked on the north side of the city. The Andaris Pavilion Building held a lot of different offices. One of them, no doubt, held Mary Stevens, and a little digging turned up news of an employee party at the building that night.

As workers started returning. I realized the party was obviously a swank affair. Fortune favored me, though. At the back of the building, a serving staff was putting trays together for the soiree. I grabbed a topcoat from the back of one of the trucks, and lent a hand bringing champagne in. I guess an exception to the elevator's exclusivity was being made for the party; I rode up the six floors with two other men who were wheeling trays of food that likely cost more than my rent.

When we got up there, I spotted Mary making small talk with some other clerk. I kept an eye on her until she left the room briefly, ditched my "work" jacket, and followed her to the powder room. Lingering outside, I button-hooked her as she came back out again.

"Miss Stevens? Mary Stevens?"

She looked surprised. "Yes?"

"My name's Sage. Marcus Sage. I'm--"

"An investigator. Yes." Her voice was icy. "I know who you are."

"Then we can dispense with some of the formalities. Mind if I ask you a few questions?"

She sighed and fished for a cigarette in her bag. "Go ahead. Free country."

I lit the smoke for her. "Kind of funny seeing you celebrating right after Mister. Liston's death."

She laughed, a sharp, bitter sound. "I'd dance on his grave. He can rot in hell for all I care."

"Funny. He seemed to think you and he had something together."

"Yeah. Obviously. That's why he hired you to follow me around."

"He told you?"

"Told me?" Her voice raised, then lowered to a hissing whisper. "He came right into the office and started waving around that dirty picture you took. Right while I'm taking dictation from my boss. He called me a whore and shoved the damn thing in my face!"

"So you'd want to see him dead?"

She glared at me. "I didn't say that."

"You're angry enough."

"I didn't *say* that. Even if I did, the cops say Howard got killed, what? Day before yesterday?"

"That's what they say."

"I was here. All day. People saw me." She gave a smug look. "You can ask my boss."

I choked back saying that maybe her boss had reason to lie for her as well. Instead, I nodded. "Let's talk to your boss, then."

The smug look continued. She nodded. "Let's go."

We walked back to the party, and once we got inside, Mary pointed. "There he is."

You could've knocked me over with a feather. Oh, sure, the fact that Mary's boss was Tilman Andaris was impressive. But that didn't floor me. What almost did was the woman on Andaris' arm.

It was Ellen.

****

Mary must've thought I was stunned by being in the presence of the richest man in Chicago. She smiled. "Yeah, so, let's go talk to him, huh? He'll vouch for me."

"That's... All right."

"Heh," she sneered, "don't want to have to explain to a man who could buy you with pocket change why you're harassing his secretary?"

I turned toward her, snapping back to the matter at hand. "No, you know what? You're right. Let's go have a chat, shall we?"

I'll admit I sounded a lot braver than I actually was, but I was in this far. Mary crossed the room, and I followed. We reached Andaris just as he was ending some anecdote for a solidly-built man.

"...I told him he had ten hours to do it. Never knew a man to book plane tickets so fast in my life."

The solidly-built man laughed, and Andaris looked the magnanimous host. Ellen... Ellen turned toward me, and the only way I could define her look was 'haunted.'

"Mister Andaris?"

Andaris looked at Mary with only a hint of recognition. The type that comes when you have so many underlings they're interchangeable to you. "Yes?"

"This is Marcus Sage."

There was a flicker of recognition in Andaris' eyes, but it faded quickly. He looked to Mary with confusion, then nodded to me, "Mister Sage."

"He's the guy who took the picture."

The penny dropped for Andaris. "Ah. Yes." He looked to Ellen. "Would you excuse us for a moment, dear?"

The "dear" chilled my blood. Ellen looked from Andaris to me and back again, then simply nodded and walked off to another part of the crowd. My eyes followed.

"Mr. Sage." Andaris's voice was quiet. "I believe you caused a bit of a problem for Miss Stevens here. You do this professionally?"

"Cause problems? Sometimes."

Mary looked angrier, but Andaris remained calm. "I'm hoping this issue can be put to rest. I know you were likely paid a good deal for those pictures. I'm willing to make a substantial offer to have you hand the copies over to me."

"I'm not for sale." I grumbled.

"I find everyone who says that just hasn't had their price met yet. I don't like to barter, and you've caused my assistant some great discomfort that I'd like to see ended for good. Eleven hundred dollars. First and final offer."

It knocked the wind out of me. That was a new car, right there. Or rent for a year. Anyone who tells you they don't think twice is lying.

Of course, my willpower had an ace in the hole: my dislike of people who see other people as pawns.

"It's a tempting offer, but I think the pictures may become evidence."

"In... what?" Andaris seemed a bit taken aback.

"Howard's dead," Mary said. If I didn't know better, there was actually a quaver in her voice.

Andaris blinked. "I'm sorry to hear that. Truly."

Mary just nodded, and I could tell that hard shell of hers was starting to crack, just a bit.

"So..." I said, trying to get things back on track, "I can't sell. But maybe things will become easier if you could vouch for Miss Stevens' whereabouts Monday morning?"

Andaris nodded. "She was taking notes at a shareholder meeting. Plenty of people there, don't need to take my word for it. Incidentally, if it turns out the photos aren't needed... My offer still stands."

I swear, Mary looked to her boss like he was the world's greatest hero. He was tossing money to me just to help save her reputation. At that point, I figured she would've done anything for him.

"Of course. I'll let you know if things change. In the meantime... a nice evening to you. Both."

"To you as well." Andaris turned and spoke quietly to Mary.

Ellen was standing across the room. She was easy to pick out; the only black woman at the party who wasn't wearing serving clothing. The white dress and gloves she wore made her look almost angelic. Before that moment, I'd thought my heart was long-dead. As I crossed the room, it was beating like Gene Krupa in overdrive.

She looked at me, and her eyes were...unreadable. There was sadness there, and... fear? I wasn't sure. Had I changed so much?

"Long time no see, doll."

She sighed. "Marcus. I-- I never thought..."

"Neither did I."

We stood in silence for a moment, each searching for words. The band struck up. I held out my hand. "May I have this dance?"

She looked over my shoulder toward where Mary and Andaris spoke. For a brief second, my jealousy of that man almost tore out of my chest. I did my best not to let it show. "So you're with him now?"

"It's... complicated," she said. And didn't I know it. Andaris was rich and powerful. The idea of a black woman attached to him would be a hard stigma to move past.

I took her gloved hand and started moving along with the others on the dance floor. We got a few glances. I didn't care, but it quickly became obvious that Ellen did.

Once I'd danced with her and it was like poetry in motion. Every move we made together was as if we'd had one body, one soul, shared between us. Now, while her movements were still precision, there was a damning awkwardness that I sensed more than saw. The others on the floor watched us, I think more for our skin color than our staggering grace.

On the second pass around the floor, Ellen broke her gaze from me.

"Marcus, please--"

"What?"

"Don't do this."

The jealousy spiked. "Don't do what? After all this time, you're leaving me with questions?"

She looked away, hurt by the accusation. "I'm sorry, Marcus. I never meant to leave you."

"But you did anyway. And now you're back. Can you at least tell me what happened?"

Her eyes met mine. Pain there, and sadness. "Don't, Marcus. Let it drop. Let it all drop. Please. If not for your own sake, then...do it for me. Just this one thing. Let it go."

A cold shiver ran down to my bones as the music stopped, but I continued to hold onto her. "Why? For the love of God, Ellen. Why?"

Her lips parted. For the life of me I wish I knew what she was going to say. Instead, I heard another voice.

"I think it's time for you to go."

I turned, and Andaris was there, along with two thick-looking men.

If she'd told me to stay, I would've beaten those two men to within an inch of their lives. I would've licked anyone who stood between us.

But it didn't happen that way.

"Please." Ellen whispered. "Just go."

My hand lingered in her glove for one more moment. I looked to her, then to Andaris, and said, "Sorry. I'm not the kind to overstay my welcome."

As I stepped towards the exit, I called back, "If things

change... I'll let you know."

"See that you do," Andaris called after me, but it wasn't him I'd been speaking to.

****

I don't relish the infidelity jobs. They always leave me feeling a little queasy. "But Marcus, you were on the front. You were at Dachau. How does something like this rattle you?" The answer is simple. If you bring your client bad news, you're the bad guy for doing so. Good news, you've wasted their money and time. It never, ever works out.

I'd timed things to trace Mary's route on her day off. I trailed her to the park across from her office where she spent her morning reading a novel. It was as innocent an outing as one could devise. Still, I stayed in the long shadow of the war memorial and snapped a few pictures as she passed by.

Noon brought her to a little café, and immediately the hairs on the back of my neck stood at attention; she'd circled the block twice before going in, as if she felt she might be followed. I'd snapped a shot of her looking furtively around while walking along the side of the building, and another of her double-checking her hair in the window next door before heading in.

I watched from just across the street as Miss Stevens walked to a table for two and sat with a young, dark-haired man. From my distance, I didn't get many details, but the lunch was a long one, and there ended up being pictures of hands being held.

When the two left, I hailed a cab and followed theirs.

They were headed into the Necropolis, which confused me a bit until they ended up at Walter and Vine. There was a small hotel there of the no-questions-asked variety. I watched from outside as the mister signed the guest book, and the two headed for the elevator.

It took the most miniscule of bribes to the desk clerk to find out which room they were in. I climbed the fire escape in back and found the room the two were sharing. The blinds were only up an inch or so, but it was enough for camera work. The couple were enthusiastic, and loud enough that the shutter-sound wasn't a problem. The pictures would tell it all. For a moment as I finished my film, I felt genuinely sorry for Mister Liston.

But a man has to eat, and sometimes a man feeds himself on the treachery in the heart of others. So it would be that Tuesday. I climbed back down the fire escape, and went back to my office to develop the pictures.

****

So I'd made a scandal, and someone got murdered for photos dealing with that scandal. I spent the entire way from the Andaris Building back to my apartment trying to figure out where to go from there. After a few hours of banging my head on the metaphorical desk, I decided it was time to talk to someone who knew more about scandal than anyone else I'd met.

****

The Blackpoole was the hottest spot in the Necropolis. It didn't look like much from the outside, but the top musicians of Chicago would give their collective left arms to play there. The place was open to everyone, black, white, living, or dead. There were scandalous rumors that the owner, Mamu Waldi, was a ghoul herself, and promoted Renfields to satisfy their unnatural lusts on the dead in her own back room. Then again, rumors say a lot of things....

The security at the front door knew me. The zombi I'd taken to calling "Fred" and the ghoul... Well, I called him Marvin because that was his name. One brainless dead, one sapient. They made quite the pair.

Fred saw me first and gave a grunt to Marvin. Marvin managed a half-smile and a wave, "Mister Sage." He said. "Mistress Waldi was expecting you."

"For real?" I asked, a little unnerved. Marvin gave his blankest stare, and I realized I wasn't going to get the full story from him.

Fred motioned me inside, and as soon as the door opened, a blast of heat billowed out like the furnaces of Hades itself. The dance floor was packed, and some clarinet player was holding everyone in sway like a snake charmer. He was good. Almost made me forget why I was there.

If Mamu was expecting me, I didn't want to make her wait. I made my way around the dance floor and gave a nod to the two living security men at the door to the back office. They'd seen me before, and let me through without question.

And the heat was gone. No matter how hot Mamu kept her club, the back office was always air conditioned and comfortably cool. It was also completely sound-proof, and as the door closed behind me the sudden switch to noiselessness threw me off-guard.

Mamu was easily one of the most gorgeous women in the Necropolis. Add to that a head for figures and a mind like a steel trap when it came to names and faces, and mix in a level of ruthlessness that a king cobra would envy, and you can understand why Mamu controlled half the sin market of the south side of Chicago.

At that moment, however, she was sitting at her desk, reading an issue of Look magazine. It looked so *normal* that I almost laughed.

Her eyes flicked up from the page. "Marcus. I heard you were around. Please, have a seat. Can I get you something to drink?"

"Scotch, thanks," I said. "I heard you were expecting me."

She laughed as she stood and poured from a small bar on the far wall. "You fell for that? Honestly, Marcus, I thought you were less of a rube."

I refused to show my embarrassment, taking the drink she offered and letting the matter drop.

"I did want to thank you," she said, sipping her own drink.

"For what?"

"Taking that bastard who ran that ... farmhouse... off the board."

The farmhouse. A slave operation for people who had appetites for young, undead flesh. The whole thing had made my skin crawl.

"Yeah, places like that..." I trailed off.

She nodded. "Besides. Bad for business."

"Take your customers?"

I immediately regretted saying that. She gave me a look that would kill a lesser man in his tracks. "It's bad for business when people outside of the Necropolis start thinking that's the kind of stuff we do here. You know I've had people from the BNA here twice in the past week? Once during business hours! They're scaring off the customers!"

"Sorry about that. Looked packed tonight..."

She sighed. "I apologize. Just ...angry. But you did take the farmhouse off the table, and I owe you for that one."

She didn't so much walk as saunter towards me, her whole body a finely crafted timepiece keeping beat with the increasing tempo of my pulse.

"And I always pay my debts. Promptly."

Mamu was right next to me, and I have to admit, if I'd not had Ellen on my mind, that would've been the end of the night for me. As it was, the temptation was awfully strong.

It took me a few seconds to get my bearings. "You know a man named Steven Waiber?"

Mamu looked only slightly disappointed. "And this is what you take for repayment?" She sighed. "All right, Marcus, but I think you got a better offer."

"And one I appreciate. This, sadly, is business."

Mamu sat on the other side of the desk and pondered for a moment. "I know a guy who uses that name, but it's not his real one."

"He's dead."

She looked completely unimpressed. "Not surprising. Low-level thugs get that way."

"Know any reason he might've been going through my office?"

She laughed. "Because Jonah Sexton told him to."

I felt a migraine coming on. "Jonah Sexton. The hit man."

"Jonah Sexton's in charge now."

I almost choked on my drink. This was bad news. Sexton had had it in for me for a long time. I hadn't kept track of where the dominoes were going to drop; I'd torn down the farmhouse out of a mixture of rage and self-preservation. The power vacuum had left Sexton in charge?

"How the hell did Sexton earn that level of power? He was a mook two months ago."

"A mook you put in jail."

"Twice. Don't remind me. He's ruthless, but he's hardly the sharpest knife in the drawer. People don't become a head man in the mob without some brains. How in the hell does a man get to that level of power that quickly?"

"Everyone knows, Sage."

"Knows what?"

Mamu raised an eyebrow. "You're just playing coy now. Sexton. Everyone knows he has a gwambi in his pocket."

I'd heard the name before. Slang for a necromancer. "You're saying that Sexton has been working with something illegal? Shocked, I tell you. I'm shocked."

Mamu shook her head, looking at me with a modicum of pity. "A gwambi, Sage, not your standard necromancer. You don't know what that means?"

"Enlighten me," I said, moving to pour another drink. As my hand reached across the bar, Mamu's clamped down on my wrist.

"Pay attention, or this lesson will be powerfully expensive, Sage."

There was a look in her eyes, something I'd never seen before. Fear. Nothing scared Mamu Waldi.

"What the hell am I getting into?"

"A gwambi is a necromancer that can use things of the dead... the names, the icons... to pick up the secrets from those beyond. Secrets have power, Sage."

"You mean he's doing some sort of séance?" I tried to scoff, but it didn't come out right. Mamu knew I was getting a little nervous as well.

"Not like that," she said, releasing my hand and pouring me a drink herself, "The gwambi know how the shadows work, how life and death work. They take things that symbolize death, and use them to ensnare souls. They're necromancers that can bring a person power. Give them their darkest wishes. Money. Fame. Love. Power..."

A successful bar carved out of the Necropolis.

I wasn't going to say it. I wouldn't insult Mamu like that. Never.

"And Sexton has one of these in his pocket."

"So they say."

"So what do I do about it?"

Mamu shrugged, "They say there are things that can protect--"

"Nothing protects from necromancy."

She incredulously arched her eyebrow again. "So you say, Sage. So I guess your only option is to be careful. Be very, very careful."

****

After I left the Blackpoole, I started putting figures together. Sadly, this wasn't an instance in which I could draw everyone together in the library and point out the killer. Libraries were in short supply, and at that point, I still wasn't sure who the "killer" was, much less what he wanted. But I was sick of waiting to see who would want me either paid off or dead next, so, as late as it was, I decided to put some bait in the water and see what came of it.

I spent the next two hours going to every dive bar in the south side, letting Sexton know, via proxy, that I had what he wanted, and that I wanted to chat. I ended up getting a lot of blank stares, and two bar-brawls, but the message got out. Now I just had to wait.

****

I got back home and had hung my hat on the hook when I heard the sound of movement in the kitchen.

Not for the last time did I curse the cops for taking my

gun. I looked around the front hall and realized that, unless my hat were suddenly to transform into cast iron, I was completely unarmed. Beyond that, the door had closed behind me; whoever was inside knew I had just come in.

So, my only choice was a frontal assault. I steeled myself for a fight, and ran headlong into the kitchen.

My momentum was stopped by the sight of Ellen sitting at the kitchen table.

"How did you get in here?"

I immediately regretted saying it. She looked hurt.

"That's the first thing you say to me?"

I pulled out the chair across from her and sat. "No. No, of course not."

She drew back her hand as I reached for it, and said quietly, "I told your neighbor we were friends from way back. You'd be proud of him. He asked me questions about you until he was satisfied."

It made me feel even worse. "I'm sorry Barney interrogated you."

She looked away. "He was trying to keep you safe. I can understand that."

There was a long silence. I had a million questions I needed to ask, and they were all jammed into the doorway of my throat, vying for which would come first. Would I lead with "what happened" or go straight to "how did you end up with Tilman Andaris instead of me?"

She knew me too well, and was merciful. "There'll be time for answers. Marcus. I missed you."

I sighed. I didn't want to hear the "but" I felt coming in

fast.

"But that time isn't now. I'm sorry... I'm so sorry."

"But there will be time?" My voice cracked a little. She was destroying me.

She reached up to touch my cheek, but her hand stopped short.

"I promise, love. I promise."

I nodded. It would have to be enough.

"Then..." *Why did you come here?* Another question I didn't want to ask. At that moment, all I wanted was to just be there, with her. Like the last five years hadn't happened. All the cynicism and gunfights and horrors... none of it.

But they had happened, and that wasn't the worst of it.

"I came to ask you to give the photos to Tilman."

Tilman. First names. As much as I hated it, I began to go from broken-sad to broken-jealous.

"Why?"

"Because it will be best, Marcus. He'll give you a lot of money--"

"Screw the money!"

Her expression changed to one of sadness. "Please, Marcus. Please. Tilman is powerful, in ways you don't even know."

"I can take care of myself."

She shook her head. "He'll hurt you, Marcus, in ways you can't even imagine."

"Let him try."

"Please, Marcus! Do this for me."

I stared at her for a long time. She was afraid. Afraid of Andaris.

After a few minutes of silence, she stood and left without a sound. I wanted to stop her, but... It was like watching my own nightmares in slow-motion. I couldn't move. My jealousy was quickly replaced with rage. I didn't know what Andaris had done to Ellen, but I began to long for a showdown with the most powerful man in the city.

****

Nightmares have followed me since the war, and while I know in the movies the hero will often wake up screaming, For me it's the opposite. I wake up paralyzed. Nightmares of Dachau will keep me immobile for a good hour, my heart pounding. That night, though, it was just Ellen walking away, over and over.

I stared at the ceiling and willed my feet and hands to do their things to no avail. Following, I did what I'd learned to do over the last few years; I waited.

In this case, waiting turned out to be the right thing. Staring at the ceiling can give a man a lot of time to focus his thoughts and think about matters at hand.

****

I'm not paranoid by nature, but in a place like the Necropolis, it pays to be a little more aware than your average Joe. Unfortunately, I'm not always on my game. I'd gone to the warehouse district to look for the photos, when half way through an alley, I heard the voice behind me.

"Don't move, Mister Sage."

I'm one to disobey orders by nature. I turned and saw Buchanan and Williams standing at the mouth of the alley. The latter was cracking his knuckles. The former held a small pistol.

"You told the cops about us, Sage. That was a poor idea," Buchanan said, shaking his head in mock sympathy.

"Did I?" I said. "Must've slipped somewhere."

"Now, normally, someone rats us out, we make them go away," he said, gesturing towards me with his pistol. He frowned as I didn't flinch.

"But you're not going to do that."

"What makes you think that?"

I shrugged. "One, if you're that worried about the cops, then you know that me ending up murdered is going to leave a trail right back to you. Two, you obviously have been trailing me, and that means you're still looking for the photos. Three, you're *talking to me about it* instead of just shooting me."

Buchanan shrugged, "Mister Williams, get the information out of Mister Sage. Don't worry about broken bones."

Amateurs. Williams came at me and blocked Buchanan's shot, which was all I needed.

Williams was a trained fighter, and I'd seen him fight, twice; he'd scored a TKO against Mac Turney, and gotten laid out by Andrew Hagar in the third. Beyond the intelligence on what he could take and what he couldn't, I had one advantage: I fight really dirty.

I ducked under Williams' meaty fist and kicked his knee. He twisted and tried to wrestle me into a bear-hug. Buchanan realized his error and screamed for Williams to get out of the way, but the below-the-belt shot I gave him made him too mad to listen.

He lumbered forward and I took a step back, then ran at him. He expected the charge and tried to grab me once again. I expected him to expect it. It gave me just enough time to hit the dirt and skid underneath him. I slugged him in the back of the knee to pitch him forward and give myself time. In a flash I had a hunk of concrete in hand which I pitched at Buchanan, knocking the gun from his hand. I leaped to my feet and charged the little man. I backhanded him with all I had. It was enough. He went sprawling.

But I still had the giant to deal with. Williams had closed the distance and gotten a hold on my shirt collar. For the first time I actually thanked the cheapness of my sartorial tastes as I lunged forward and the bit of fabric came off in the boxer's meaty hand.

His eyes and mine locked on Buchanan's gun, now stuck under the edge of a trashcan. We both lunged. Him for the gun, me for the can. I swung the full trash bin in an uppercut-arc, and nailed Williams right in the jaw as he was leaning down. He flew backward like a cartoon character, and smacked against the alley wall, sliding down into unconsciousness. I'd scored a first-round KO.

****

I slapped Buchanan awake, the muzzle of his gun pressed to his cheek. His eyes went wide.

"Oh God, Sage! Don't kill me!"

"Why did Sexton send you for the photos?"

"He didn't!"

"Liar!"

"No! Listen to me! He wants 'em, sure, but I figured we'd get 'em and sell 'em to him!"

"What does he want them for?"

"I don't know!"

"I'm losing my patience!"

I placed my knee on his chest to stop his squirming. Leaning in caused him to gasp for breath.

"Okay, okay! He's got some kinda beef about a necromancer--"

"A gwambi."

Buchanan's eyes went wide. I knew I'd hit the mark.

He nodded. "Yeah. One of those. He's trying to get something over on Tilman Andaris!"

It was like Christmas and Easter all in one. Sexton had a gwambi pointed at Andaris, and my photos were somehow the missing piece of the puzzle that might take the big man out. I could only barely suppress my grin as I continued on with Buchanan.

"You've been straight with me, Buchanan. I'm gonna let you go. But if you come after me again, with or without that garbage truck you call a fighter, they'll never find your body. Get it?"

Buchanan nodded. "Sure, Sage! Any--"

I clocked him with the gun, sending him back into blackness. Didn't have to. Just wanted to.

****

After grabbing the photos from the warehouse, I took the rolled-up envelope and high-tailed it to a greasy spoon about a half-mile away. There, a new girl brought my coffee and, almost immediately after, my burger. I sat in the booth, nursed my coffee, and took out the photos.

It had started innocently enough. Following Mary to the park, then the café. There was a kiss or two there, a holding-of-hands, but it was still pretty chaste. The sleazy stuff happened after they got to the hotel. I noted the one picture that Liston had taken with him; the couple half-naked and embracing as they moved to the fully-unclothed state. It was incriminating, sure, but... Mary had been pretty open about her affair after the photos were shown to her, and her fiancé was no longer a problem. A secretary looks for a little extra romance in the afternoon? How would a gwambi use that against Andaris?

It had to be something else. I took out my loupe and examined the photos.

"What're you doing?"

I looked up at the waitress, and realized that "none of your business" wouldn't be a good line to throw at her. She had the good grace to look sheepish at interrupting me, and reddened as she saw some of the more salacious pictures strewn over the table. Still, she didn't leave immediately. Either she had a lot of moxie, or she was paralyzed with embarrassment. Alternatively, she just wanted to refill my coffee.

I slid my cup over to give her the out, and she didn't take it, so I explained. "I'm a private eye, I've been checking some photos for a case. Just going over the details."

She gave a nod towards the photos in the park. "My brother's on that."

I frowned. "The picture?"

She pointed more directly, "The war memorial."

I grabbed my loupe and nodded, "Some of my friends, too."

She gave me a sad smile. "PFC Simon Bakeland."

I started scanning the pictures for the name. Something else caught my eye and I paused. I scanned again.

I took out the rest of the park pictures and looked them over closely.

"Something wrong?"

I dropped the loupe back in my pocket, "Maybe. Thanks, doll, you may've just been my compass." I took out the remaining money from my wallet, sans bus fare, and left it on the table. Scooping up the pictures, I half-ran out the door.

****

"Hey Mamu. You got a minute?"

"For you, Sage? All the time in the world."

I could hear the grin in her voice, but once again, I didn't have time for flirtation.

"You told me about gwambis before, about how they can get power from names."

Her voice became cold and guarded. "Yes. That I did. The names of the dead."

"Would they actually have to have a physical representation of the name? Like taking a tombstone or something?"

"They wouldn't need that if they were working small-time, but having that would be very, very powerful indeed."

"Powerful enough to control a relative of the dead?"

A long pause. "Why are you asking this, Sage?"

"Just answer!"

"Yes, maybe. If the relative was close and the emotional tie between the two was strong. Sage, I'm beginning to get concerned. What's going on?"

"Look, Sexton is still after me. Can you buy me some time?"

"You'll owe me another one. You know that."

"I'll owe you a boatload if I can pull this off."

"I'll do what I can, Sage, but remember... I will collect."

"I know, Mamu. Thanks."

****

By the time I got to the park, the streetlights were coming on. I made a beeline to the war memorial. A cop who likely didn't like the cut of my jib came up after me and asked, "There a problem, boyo?"

I shook my head, then motioned him closer as I caught my breath. "You do this beat a lot?"

"Every day for the past six years."

I nodded and pointed at the memorial. "That new?"

He saw what I was pointing to, and cursed quietly. "Young hooligans. Place like this deserves more respect than this. Probably happened in the last couple of weeks. How'd you know?"

I looked at the gouged-out section of the plaque where a nameplate was now missing. "Lucky guess."

The cop shook his head. "Just move along. I'll make a report of it."

I nodded. Buchanan had been completely wrong about the blackmail angle. Sexton's gwambi had been there all right, and he'd taken a very specific name. He had gained himself a powerful link from PFC Jack Brody, brother of Hollis Brody, the local director of the Bureau of Necromantic Affairs.

****

I got back to my place and just stared at the pictures for

a half-hour. This was bad. This was tremendously bad. Sexton's gwambi now had hold over the head of the Chicago BNA. As much as that organization had become a pain in the collective ass of the Necropolis, Brody was a good man. He'd saved my life more than once, and he was doing good work. If Sexton already controlled him... I thought about the rumors that BNA agents were grabbing people out of their own homes not that far away from where I lived. I didn't want to think about it, but it wouldn't go away.

The phone rang, and I picked it up. "Marcus here."

"I know that, darling. You weren't at your office." Mamu was on the other end of the line. "Who do you love, darling?"

I was so deep in thought, it took me a moment to swim back to the surface. The only word that came out in response at first was, "Huh?"

"Who do you love? I'll give you a hint. She's gorgeous, owns the hottest club in the Necropolis, and you owe her a favor."

I frowned and leaned forward, putting the photo down. "I don't have time for this, Mamu."

She made a disappointed sound, and if anything, her tone grew more teasing. "Spoilsport."

"What do you want?"

"You know how you wanted a meeting with Sexton? I've made it for you, darling."

I paused. Something was up.

"You still there?"

"Yeah. What's in this for you?"

"Nothing, darling. Well, other than you owing me another favor, and me helping keep peace in Dodge, so-to-speak."

"You've got a heart of gold now?"

She chuckled. "You're assuming I ever had a heart. Now, come on over here, and bring the photographs. Ed and Milton will let you in the front. Don't keep me waiting, Sage."

The line went dead, and after I hung up, I immediately checked the clip on Buchanan's pistol. Mamu had misnamed not one, but both of her doormen. Something was wrong, someone was listening in, and she definitely wanted me to know both those facts.

****

I got to the Blackpoole twenty minutes later. Neither Fred nor Marvin (or, I guess, "Ed" or "Milton") were at the front door. Instead, two no-neck types who were obviously packing hardware gave me the predator's own eyeball and nodded at me to head in.

I cruised into the back room. The chill of the air conditioning was working overtime, but that wasn't the only thing that had me shivering.

Mamu was sitting in her chair on the far side of the desk. Her lip was split, and she had a cut over her left eye. She looked like every ounce of her blood had been replaced with raw hatred and fury.

Standing a few feet to her left and right were goons with their pistols drawn, and sitting on the corner of the desk was Sexton.

Sexton had worked his way up the mob food chain by bumping off people who got in a little too deep. His preferred method of destruction was strangulation, and his work had given him hands not unlike two freight cars. He looked at me through a mop of unkempt hair, and grinned.

"So, shamus. I hear you've been wanting to talk."

"You know, you could've just stopped by the office."

He chuckled. "Not my style, shamus. And I figure by now you know how valuable my time is. Besides, you owe me one for the elimination of my mook."

"The so-called 'Waiber.'"

He nodded. "That's him."

"I don't suppose it matters that I didn't kill him, and that even if I did, he was breaking into my place."

Sexton shook his head, "Doesn't matter in the slightest. He was in your place, stabbed with your letter opener. You owe me. You're not going to disappoint me, are you?"

"I'll try not to," I said, and started to sit with deliberate slowness. "Lemme ask one thing, though... You shot Liston?"

Sexton smirked and gave me the go-ahead nod to sit, "My boys did. We thought he had all the photos. Unlucky him. You *have* brought the pictures, right?"

"Before I answer that, could you at least tell me what the gwambi's name is?"

Sexton froze for a moment. "Lots of big questions for such a small man. I'd ask where you learned about gwambis, but..." His eyes drifted toward Mamu, who stared daggers at him.

"Okay, if not that, tell me how you think you're going to survive this?"

Sexton glared, and walked over, placing his hand on my shoulder. I winced as he started to crush with his grip. One of my tendons popped. "You think you're in some position to threaten me, shamus? Where are the photos?"

It looked like witty banter wasn't going to work this time. "Okay, okay!" I said. "They're out in my car!"

Sexton looked to his boys. One of them ran out of the office, heading toward the front door. Sexton's hand continued to crush.

"You better not be lying to me, shamus."

I shook my head, "You know the photos won't save you from Andaris. He'll figure out who your gwambi is, and he'll wring your neck with that until you're either dead or just another pawn of his."

The reaction was not what I'd expected. Sexton just stared at me for a long moment, then laughed. "I heard you were smart, Sage. Not this time. You got it all backward. Thing is, anyone who knows about any of this gets a one-way trip south. And now that you've spilled your guts in front of the witch here," he angled his head toward Mamu, "she's gonna have to get real quiet, too. Shame, really." He turned and looked her way. "I was going to have some fun with her."

"I'd rather sleep with a rot zombi." Mamu hissed. "Though from what I hear, you're just as deficient."

He turned and raised his hand to strike her, and that was the moment I needed.

When you're fighting for your life, all bets are off. There's no honor that will protect you from buying a cemetery plot. I'm not proud of it, but from behind, I kicked Sexton hard in the crotch.

As he pitched forward, Mamu dove for the gun-hand of the remaining thug. I went for my pistol, but Sexton slapped my hand aside, and the gunshot went wild as the gun was knocked from my hand. Thinking of the thugs out front, I was suddenly very, very happy that Mamu's office was so well sound-proofed.

But Sexton was atop me, choking me. I reached for the pistol, and spots danced in my vision. Sexton's eyes were wide and furious, and I couldn't get my arm to stretch that extra inch.

There was a click, and suddenly Sexton's grip loosened. I couldn't see until he rolled off of me, but Mamu was now standing with a pistol pointed at his head, the hammer cocked back.

"Nice shot, Sage." Her face was still pure anger, but I could tell she was relieved. In the corner, I saw the thug my stray shot had killed.

Mamu glared. "You have a very bad penance coming from this, Sexton."

"Later," I said. "His other boy will be coming back after he figures out I didn't drive here."

Sexton chuckled, "You're never gonna get out of here alive."

I stared him in the eye and growled, "What did you mean that I got it all backward?"

He laughed, "Not so smart after all, are you, spook?"

I made to kick him, but Mamu shook her head. "No, wait."

I wondered what she wanted to bring up. Turns out she just wanted to kick him before I could. And if I thought my groin-shot was vicious, I suspect Mamu left Sexton a permanent soprano.

****

We left Sexton unconscious. To be fair, he hadn't started that way, but I got in a few good hits. I told myself it was necessary, but in the end, Mamu saw me grin a little. She frowned, and handed me the gun she'd been threatening Sexton with.

I tried to give it back. "You're gonna need this."

She shook her head, and walked back to the other side of the desk. From out of a drawer came a wicked-looking obsidian knife. Just looking at it gave me the shivers.

Her voice was as cold as any stone. "This should do fine."

"Just don't do anything foolish."

"They came to my house, Sage. Violated my peace. Hurt my people. I don't think anything I could do right now would be called 'foolish.'"

She was right, and I knew it, but... I walked to her side of the desk, and looked her in the eye. "Don't do anything that will get you killed."

Her smile returned, and she reached up with her free hand to caress my face, "Why Sage, I didn't know you cared."

Before I could say anything more, she was already half way across the room. The door popped open, and the goon who'd been sent outside took one step in.

"Boss, I couldn't--"

His eyes went wide as Mamu slashed his throat. He crumpled with a wordless rattle escaping his lips. Mamu muttered something under her breath and spat at his fallen form, then stepped out into the club. I followed.

The two at the door must've sensed something. They ran in, immediately ducking behind tables.

"Boss? BOSS?"

"He's in the back," I called. "Go ahead and check for yourself."

"You son of a bitch spook!" one of the other men yelled, and a few shots thudded into the table I'd quickly hidden behind.

I heard something thud, then more gunshots, then a panicked scream. I stuck my head out quickly, and what I saw did my heart a world of good. Mamu had managed to get her doormen out from wherever the goons had locked them up. Fred and Marvin had closed on the two goons at the door, and the mooks learned that a few small-caliber bullets to the body don't bother zombis much at all.

I popped off a few more shots to keep the final gunman down. "Throw down the gun, and I'll make sure Fred and Marvin don't tear your arms off. Deal?"

There was a half-second pause, and the goon's gun flew to the center of the dance floor. He stood, raised his hands, and gave me a pleading look. "Okay, I surrender! I surrender!"

I was about to give him terms, but Mamu snaked up behind him faster than I expected. I yelled, "No!" But it was too late. His throat opened like a bloody smile.

"No!" I yelled again. "That wasn't the deal!"

"I didn't see my men touch his arms," Mamu said coldly. "My house. My peace. My people."

I shivered. I'd always known Mamu was tough, and not to be crossed, but beyond handling drunks and people who owed her favors or money, I'd never seen her reputation in action. A line had been crossed. I only hoped she would cross it back again.

"Let me call the cops on Sexton."

She frowned. "The cops don't care. He's got them in his pocket. You know that."

I nodded. She was right. "Let me call someone else, then."

Her eyes narrowed. "Look me in the eye and tell me who."

I sighed. She'd suspected. "The BNA."

"No." Her voice was like a thunderbolt. "They do not step in this place. Not now. Not ever again."

"Mamu, I need information from Sexton. I can't let you kill him."

There was a long pause. Mamu sized me up through narrowed eyes. I never felt so naked in my life.

"Very well," she said. She slid the knife into a slit in her dress, and it disappeared into a garter that, another time, would've been more than a little arousing. "Bring him out. We will get the truth. But after that... he's mine."

I guess the pain and the adrenaline were still buzzing; I didn't shiver at what Mamu had said. I simply nodded and retrieved Sexton.

Dragging him into the main room, I saw Mamu sitting at one of the tables ringing the dance floor as if nothing had happened. I slapped Sexton a couple of times, and his eyes flickered open. As he regained consciousness, I stepped back and pointed Buchanan's pistol at his chest.

"Let's try this again. How did I 'get it all backward'?"

"Fuck you, spook."

"This ain't a popgun I got here, punk."

Sexton shook his head. "It's you killin' me now or them later."

There was someone Sexton feared more than a guy with a gun to his chest? This was bad news, and I was getting a real sinking feeling.

"Yeah, you're right," I bluffed. "I'd just kill you. She, on the other hand..."

Sexton's eyes followed mine to Mamu's. Her blade was out again, and though it was suspiciously clean, Sexton panicked at the sight of it.

"No, no, wait! I can't tell you! I can't!"

"You can and you will," Mamu said, her voice quiet. "You'll tell him all about your gwambi."

"I don't have a goddamn gwambi!"

I froze. Sexton wouldn't bluff. Not at a time like this. It

was falling into place.

"It wasn't yours. It was Andaris'."

"Please!" he whimpered, "I can't! The gwambi's got my name!"

"You'll tell the BNA everything you know about it. They'll protect you," I lied. I was feeling sick to my stomach now.

"No."

Mamu shook her head. "My house, Sage. My house, my people. He's mine now."

"Dammit! Sage, help me!"

Mamu stared at Sexton like a butcher sizing up a steer.

The good-cop, bad-cop routine was working. The problem was, I wasn't sure Mamu saw it as a routine. "Give me something, Sexton. Written statement. We'll take down Andaris and make sure you're protected."

There was silence. I looked down, and the mob boss' eyes were wide with an unhealthy green glow. I had no idea what was going on.

"Saaaaage..." He gasped, and then started retching and coughing. I looked to Mamu. Her eyes were wide, but unsurprised.

"Help me!" I cried out. Blood poured out from between Sexton's lips. I hauled him to his feet. He coughed up one huge chunk of blood and tissue, and then collapsed.

Now I was mad. "What did you do?" I snarled, glaring at Mamu.

"It wasn't me, Sage." As she said it, I knew it was so. "I

would've loved to make him pay, but that sort-of magic? I don't know if even the best gwambi couldn't do that. I don't know what you're facing now, Sage. I don't know at all."

"Dammit, Mamu, Sexton was my trump card!"

"What do you want me to say, Sage? You had to know that whoever was behind all this, there was no way they were going to let Sexton talk. You had to know that!"

I wanted to tell her that she should've said something before, but she was right. I had myself to blame; but while Sexton's blood was on my shirt, metaphorically it was on the hands of Andaris and whatever twisted bit of necromancy he'd turned up. One more thing to take the big man down for. I thought about the power of the unidentified gwambi in the photo who'd been taking the name off the war memorial, and I thought about how Tilman Andaris had his hooks in every crooked deal in the city. One way or another, I was going to have to go after not one, but two of the most powerful men in Chicago. There was no way I could just storm into them; I'd end up like Sexton, or worse. But I had to do *something*.

****

I mopped my brow as I crossed the street to the Americana Building. It was almost five in the morning, and the city was still hot enough to melt lead. The Americana, however, had air conditioning, and that made it a perfect place for me. For Andaris, the choice was easier; he owned the building. I knew that when I called him and asked for the meeting.

There were two goons out front, both sweating like they

were taking their own personal Turkish baths in the pre-dawn light. A quick frisk, and the removal of my pistol, got me past the human watchdogs.

Opening the door, I was hit with frigid air. Despite the pleasant temperature change, I felt ill-at-ease. I had one shot to make this right, and the timing had to be perfect.

I walked to the third door on the right. Past the smoked glass was Andaris' lounge, all tables and soft leather couches. I stepped through the door, and a light clicked on from one of the end-tables. In the pool of warm light sat Tilman Andaris. As always, he looked immensely pleased with himself. Standing just behind the couch, almost like a servant awaiting orders, was Ellen. She wouldn't meet my gaze.

For a moment, all I could hear was the blowing of the air conditioning and the rumble of the early-morning traffic passing by outside. Andaris looked at me, as if waiting for something, and then sighed. "All right, I'd hoped this would be more of a friendly chat. Please, have a seat."

"I'll stand, thanks."

"Difficult to the end. But it is the end. This one little thing, and then we can both make our wishes come true by never having to deal with each other again. You brought the pictures?"

I nodded, "You'll have them by the time we're done here."

Andaris raised an eyebrow, "Cryptic. Understand that you're still getting paid what I offered you before. You'll soon be a wealthy man. There is no twist here. No double-deal. Not from me at least."

He reached into his jacket, and, to my credit, I didn't

tense up. I didn't figure Andaris would be the kind of guy to make that little speech of his and then shoot me. Instead, he took out a thick envelope.

"You can count it if you like."

"It's not what I'm here for."

Andaris went back to his semi-astonished eyebrow raising. "It's a little late to up your price, Mister Sage. You asked for this meeting."

"I don't want your money."

Andaris frowned. "Then what is it you do want?"

I looked over his shoulder, "I want her."

Andaris turned his head to gaze past Ellen, as if there might be another "her" in the room. He then looked at her, and then at me.

"You're not serious, are you?"

"I'm more serious than polio."

He cracked a smile. "You want to purchase Miss Smith?"

"No," Ellen whispered. "Please don't... Marcus, please don't..."

"No 'sale', Tilman," I growled under my breath. "I want you to let her go. Whatever hold you have on her, I want it gone. Whatever blackmail you have, destroyed."

Andaris looked at me in disbelief. Then he started to laugh.

"Oh Mister Sage. I thought you were a man of ambition. Now I see you're a fool."

My teeth ground. "You want the pictures, you let her go."

He shook his head. "I knew you lived in the Necropolis. I never took you for a Renfield."

The word hit me like a punch to the gut. I tried to figure out what he must've really said. It couldn't be...

...And then I looked Ellen in the eyes. This is why she was staying away. This is why she wanted me to be no part of this.

Ellen looked down, ashamed of everything that had happened. Andaris stood and tucked the envelope back in his jacket, then walked to the bar, "You didn't know, did you? That's amusing. Best detective in the Necropolis, specialist with undead matters, and you didn't know."

Andaris walked to Ellen's side, "But you know what amuses me more?"

He grabbed Ellen's arm roughly. She cried out, and it was all I could do to keep from jumping him on the spot. He grinned at me.

"What really amuses me is that you thought you could hurt me with pictures that show some idiot necromancer vandalizing a monument."

He stepped around the couch, his grip still tight on Ellen's arm, and continued, "You thought you could do anything to me. Who were you going to tell? Where were you going to go? You must know, Sage, that I have a gwambi that holds the reins to the head of the BNA. I'm so deep in the police department I could have you locked away just for existing. I made you a generous offer, you knocked it away because you didn't like the way I treated some ghoul bitch? You insult me, Sage. And normally, insults from little people like you I just ignore. But you decided to make this a personal matter.

"At this moment I'm trying to decide whether to give her to you, or have Frank and Danny come in here, beat the shit out of you while she watches, then toss your broken corpse into the lake...

"Or maybe I'll have my necromancer bring you back. The two of you could be together without complications then. Of course, you'd be a mindless husk... You slapped away my generous offer, I'm not about to spring the extra money to keep your intelligence. How does that sound, Sage? Happily ever after beyond the grave?"

I barely heard a word of his rant. Ellen wouldn't look at me. She wouldn't look at me.

Andaris went further on his journey from jovial to enraged. "You want her? Fine."

Ellen yelped as Andaris all but threw her at my feet. "You know how little I value your life, Sage. The photos, and you can at least walk out of here still breathing."

I offered Ellen my hand. For the longest moment, she didn't move. Finally, her fingers entwined with mine. They were ice cold.

But then her eyes met mine. For a moment all I could see was us in them. The memories of spring days, the plans we once had.

Those plans might never have been, but I knew right then and there, whether we had a future or not, she was walking out of there.

"So," Andaris said. "You have what you want, Sage. The photos. Now."

I brought Ellen to her feet. The only sound was the rush of the air conditioning. Somewhere outside, a truck rumbled by, and a car horn honked.

"Give me a minute," I said.

"No. No more 'minutes' Mister Sage. Either you produce those pictures, or I call Frank and Danny in here."

I put an arm around Ellen and looked at the door. Andaris must've thought I was getting nervous about Frank and Danny, but his thoughts turned to confusion as the over-muscled pair burst into the room unbidden.

"Boss!" Frank said.

"You gotta see this!" added Danny. He strode across the room, and handed his boss a newspaper.

"Morning edition," I grinned, "right on time."

Andaris' face turned red, "What the..."

The pictures were right there. The necromancer, the monument, and above it in huge type,:

PRIVATE EYE FINGERS NECROMANCER.
CITY HIGER-UPS IMPLICATED!

I locked eyes with the most powerful man in the city. "There's your photos, you son of a bitch. I hope you choke on them."

Andaris looked like he was about to have a heart attack. He looked to Danny and Frank and bellowed, "What the hell are you two waiting for? Kill him!"

Frank was still next to me. I hauled off with a right cross that went from New York to San Fran. I likely busted my fingers, but he staggered back, tripping over his own feet and landing in a heap. My gun flew from his fingers, and skidded under the bar. I'd have to do this unarmed.

A kick to the ribs gave Frank something more to think about. I tried to put my fist into Danny's face next, but the goon was smart; he backpedaled and went for his jacket. I lunged at him, hoping to grab his arm.

I hadn't counted on Andaris getting his own hands dirty in this fight. He body-checked me, and, thrown off balance, I almost fell onto the couch. It was all the time Danny needed to get the gun out.

The huge automatic leveled at me, and I heard Andaris say, "Goodbye, Mister Sage."

But the gunshot never came. Danny howled and dropped, a huge bloodstain spreading between his shoulder blades. Ellen stood behind him, a bloody blade in her hand, glaring first at him, and then at Andaris.

I didn't have time to celebrate my fortune. Andaris was going for Danny's gun, but I got there first. I clicked back the hammer, and he held up his hands.

"No need to be hasty here!" He opened his jacket to indicate the envelope of money, "After all, you did get me the photos... In your own way."

I raised the pistol. "You know what amuses me? That after all this, you think a big man like you can somehow buy a little man like me. I know you've always had it that way, Andaris, but not today. Not today, and never, ever me."

A better man would've simply walked away. I'm not a

better man. I let the hammer release slowly, then pistol-whipped Andaris across the face once, just for good measure.

I looked to Ellen. "We're walking out of here."

She nodded and made for the door. I snagged my own gun from under the bar and followed, taking one last look at Andaris before we retreated.

As we hit the front door, I could hear Andaris screaming at Frank, "Kill him, you idiot!"

Ellen and I ran out into the steamy morning. The sun was just rising like a blood-red ball over the horizon. Across the street, in a Packard with the engine running, was Barney.

Ellen and I slid into the back seat, and Barney looked back. "I saw the newspaper van, I hit the horn. Did it work out?"

I nodded. "Get us the hell out of here, Barney!"

Barney didn't need to be told twice. He slammed on the gas, and in no time we were out into the early-morning traffic, heading back to the Necropolis.

****

Barney was driving like the devil and making sure we weren't being followed. In the back... I was looking at Ellen, and she at me. A moment that seemed to last for hours passed, and then she fell against me, her arms around me and mine around her. Something caught in her throat, and it took me a moment to realize what the noise was; ghouls can't make tears. They can't cry.

I held her as if somehow I could erase everything that had happened to her. Her breath was cold in my ear, "Marcus... He's never going to let us go..."

"It'll be okay," I said, not believing it myself. I'd be a fool to think, even if the law and the papers eviscerated him, that we'd ever be safe.

She pressed her forehead into mine. The terror was starting to leave her eyes, but she moved forward with a new hesitancy, "I'm sorry I didn't..."

"No words," I said to her. I so wanted this to be right, and a moment later, when she kissed me, it was.

For a moment.

Our lips parted, and I spoke. "How much hold does his necromancer have on you?"

"None. Nothing at all."

I sighed. Sometimes necromancers controlled their dead completely; it was harder to do on ghouls, but from the type of power I'd seen this one exhibit...

"He never touched me, Marcus. Never."

I drew away from her, and she looked at me questioningly. "Marcus, what's the matter?"

I wanted this not to happen. Every moment was turning everything I'd worked for into a nightmare happening in slow motion. But the truth had to come out.

I took Ellen's handbag from her. A quick rummage through it brought out the blood-stained blade she'd placed between Danny's shoulder blades.

She still looked confused. "I had to stop him, Marcus. He was going to shoot you."

"That wasn't the only person you've used it on. I don't know if you got there first and Waiber surprised you, or if you came in after he did and knew you had to get rid of him. Either way you weren't armed, so you went for this."

I turned the blade over in my hand. It was the missing letter opener from my desk.

Ellen's voice trembled as she said, "It was self-defense. I didn't even know it was your office until I got there..."

"It doesn't matter, Ellen." I wished it was true. "You might've been acting in self-defense, but you were still breaking into my office for Andaris, and you still killed a man."

"Marcus--"

"And after all that has happened, the DA isn't going to leave any stone unturned."

"I swear I didn't know."

I'd walked away from Ellen once, and it had torn my heart out. Right now, she needed someone to protect her, but the law and the papers were going to be all over me, and I'd just put a shiny bulls-eye on my back for anyone who wanted to earn favor with Tilman Andaris.

The only way I could protect her now was by walking away again.

We were pulling up to my home, and I swallowed every last bit of love I had for the woman who'd made me brave enough to take on Andaris. I made my gaze as steely as I could as I drew away from her.

"You're a killer, Ellen. You don't have the excuse that you were under the control of a necromancer, and there are going to be people looking for you. Big people, with badges. I won't protect you."

To my credit, my voice didn't waver, even once.

"So that's how it's to be?" There was so much fear and need in her voice that I had to summon every ounce of strength I had not to hold her.

"Barney will take you to the train station."

I took out the envelope of Andaris' cash, "This'll set you up. A new place, a new name."

I stepped out of the car, and words wouldn't come. Barney started up the car. The last thing I heard was that little catch in Ellen's throat: Ghouls can't cry, but as I kept my own tears in check, I wondered if I was even less alive than she was.

****

Two days later the papers had nothing but the fallout of my revelation. I'd locked my door and drawn my blinds from all of the attention I was getting. My name was bandied about because the head of the BNA had been in trouble, and the necromancer who had been targeting him had been unmasked by my deeds. There were things that were left out of the story; that the evidence had come from an adultery job, that at least three people had died in the whole fiasco, and that the newly-brewing mob war in the Necropolis had anything to do with the case.

The last thing that was left out was that Tilman Andaris was connected to it. Somehow he'd managed to shovel the blame to a local senator, who was now in custody. I didn't know how that dance had worked out, and I didn't want to know. Once again, Andaris had used his power and influence to make sure none of the shrapnel from the city's wars touched him at all. My blood boiled when I saw the picture of Andaris and BNA Director Brody shaking hands.

Barney had been exactly what I needed him to be throughout all this: quiet. He hadn't told the press anything, or even indicated he'd been part of it. He hadn't told me anything about Ellen beyond that he'd made sure she got a ticket at the train station. He'd listened to me ranting and swearing in a drunken stupor for the following two days, and made sure I both ate and slept, and he kept the press away from my front door as much as he could. There ought to be medals for that kind of person.

On the third day I woke, hung over, to knocking at the door. For a moment I considered the idea that it was Andaris' goons, but they wouldn't have knocked. Still, just to be safe, I went armed.

The sunlight blasted in and reminded me what daylight thinks of drunks. I shielded my eyes and managed to focus on the well-dressed man on my doorstep.

"Marcus Sage?"

"Only if you're my fifth-grade teacher."

He didn't crack a smile. Instead, he handed me an envelope.

"Am I being summoned for something?" I asked, starting to tear it open.

"Yes, but likely not what you think."

"I think nothing."

He didn't go for the obvious softball. He just stood there as I blearily tried to understand what I was reading. Finally, he offered some assistance.

"Make sure you're considerably cleaner than you are now tomorrow morning, Mister Sage. A car will be coming."

"You're joking."

The blood drain from my face as I read the crisply worded letter; the words that would change my life forever.

"I don't joke, Mister Sage. You're being recruited as a special resource to the Bureau of Necromantic Affairs."

Necropolis Episode 3
The Dead of the Night

It had only been a week and a half since I'd opened the door to a case that had found me knee-deep in the mob, surrounded by undead, and searching for a forbidden piece of Nazi occult lore. Ten days. It had seemed like an eternity. In that time I'd been beaten, shot at, lied to, grabbed by the cops, stiffed out of fees, and, to top it all off, I'd gotten my picture in the paper.

Sadly, it was that last bit that I wished had never happened.

Three days previous I'd tried to kick a serious dent in the fender of one of the most powerful men in Chicago. I was punching above my weight class, and I knew it, but I had to try. In the end, a necromancer he'd had in his pocket had been taken in, but Tilman Andaris had used his wealth and position to remain distanced from any appreciable fallout. I'd annoyed him, though, and that made me a new target for his wrath.

The local branch of the Bureau of Necromantic Affairs realized I'd done them a good turn by getting their director (and friend of mine) Hollis Brody out from under the thumb of said necromancer, and thus they'd decided to protect me, in their own way, from Andaris' vengeance. When the bust against the wanted necromancer had gone down, they'd made sure that the papers knew it was me who'd put the pieces together and made it happen.

Newspapers can do wonders for one's reputation. I'd

been named a "special resource" of the BNA, and it had been done in the public eye. If something happened to me, Mister Andaris would have explaining to do to the feds. It had worked out well for the BNA; they now had a tighter leash on Andaris, and they had me protected. They told me I should be grateful.

That wasn't happening.

On the tenth day after the sky started falling on me, I arrived at my office to find a bag of dead rats on my stoop. This would be the second time that had happened, and it let me know very succinctly how my neighbors felt about me.

I didn't blame them. For years after the Nazis had unleashed the secrets of necromancy into the world, the Necropolis on the south side of Chicago had become home to displaced undead persons of all stripes. The neighborhood had been a powder keg, to be sure, but we kept things largely under control, and quiet enough that the BNA never stuck their noses in.

That had changed only a week ago, but it had changed with a vengeance. The BNA, rumor had it, had been hassling people and taking citizens off the streets of the Necropolis. Now I was part of the BNA. I was part of the problem.

I spent the better part of the day in my office doing nothing. The heat was still oppressive. It was never this hot in late October. It was almost as if nature itself was angry at me for having taken up the BNA banner.

I sweated through her wrath in the afternoon, and by the time my shirt was soaked, I figured it was time to call it a day. I'd just finished locking up my file cabinet when there came a knock at the door. Knowing that I had nothing else on my plate, I sat back in my chair and reminded myself to be polite to whoever walked in, whatever they wanted; I needed the case.

"Come in," I beckoned.

The door opened with the hesitancy I'd expected. On the other side was a man, I'd say about five foot six. His suit was well-pressed, and he had that blond-haired, blue-eye'd quality that had been all the rage overseas not that long ago.

"Excuse me, are you Marcus Sage?"

"The one and only. Please, come in, Mister...?"

"Billings. Waldo Billings."

"Billings. Please come in Mister Billings."

He took the invitation and sat down in the creaky wooden chair opposite me. "I have a problem and... Well.. Do you do... fidelity work?"

I nodded. My last big case had exploded messily from fidelity work. I silently prayed that whatever Billings would give me would be much more straightforward.

"You see," he continued, "I have this... problem."

He was choosing his words carefully and slowly. If I didn't speed him up, we'd be there until the next day. I took a bottle from my lowest desk drawer along with two glasses, and motioned for him to go on as I poured us both some whiskey.

"I trust Beverly. I really, really do."

I pushed the glass across the desk and made a toasting motion. Mechanically, he took the drink and upended it.

"But you'd like someone to be sure."

He finished his drink and sighed. "Yes. That. I just..."

I held up a hand. I'd heard this story enough times, "Beverly is... your fiancée?"

"Something like that."

"Give me her address, or the address where she spends most of her time. I get five dollars a day, and I can't guarantee this will end in any pretty way."

For a moment, his lip twitched into something that was almost a grin, but it passed too quickly for me to tell. He nodded, his eyes downcast, and said, "Just get whatever you can, Mister Sage. I'd appreciate it. About how long will this take?"

"Four days." I estimated. I didn't have a hard-and-fast schedule for snoop and snitch, but four days was a typical amount. I just wanted this client interview to be over, and I'd rather Billings not dicker over the bill.

He nodded and took a crisp twenty dollar bill out of his pocket as if he knew I'd be asking for that much. He laid it on the table, "Is advance payment good?"

I held myself back from lunging for the bill; it wouldn't put forth the controlled, hard-nosed exterior I liked to create. "That would be fine," I said evenly.

"And will there be expenses?" he asked.

"There might be."

He took out another twenty and laid it atop the first one. "That should handle them?"

"That should handle them quite well. I'll write up a contract after you've given me the details."

The details were quick in coming. Billings still wouldn't

say "fiancée," but he did reveal that this Beverly McDaniels had been his "girl" for almost four months, and that he was now worried she was stepping out on him. She'd been gone for a few weekends, and couldn't really account for where she'd been. It sounded fishy to him. I had to agree with his piscine assessment.

With the contract signed, Mister Billings bade me a good day and left. I closed up shop for the night after that, and began walking home. I figured the farther I got away from my office, the fewer dirty looks I'd get. News travels fast in the jungle, and already some of the people on my block were avoiding me like the plague. I hoped they didn't have rats they would be willing to put in bags for my front step.

About half way home, I paused. There was something on the wind that made my nose twitch. I turned north and started following a burning smell. About a block and a half down from the elevated train line, I turned west, and saw it.

People were fleeing from a burning building. I immediately felt sick to my stomach; not two weeks ago I had thought I'd ended the string of zombi arsons in the city by stumbling upon the very undead creature who'd been doing them. It seemed I'd counted my chickens long before hatching day.

I ran down the street, hoping there was something I could do to help whoever might still be there. The air was acrid with the smell of burning flesh, a scent I knew all too well, and I could hear screams. A child was on the sidewalk, crying and pointing, trying to get words out about whatever loved one was in there.

I increased my pace and tore my jacket off. Just as I got to the front of the building, though, the apartment gave a sickening, maddening crunch and leaned over with a deadly slowness, as if bowing to the streetlights. Then it collapsed in on itself, spraying hot ash and sparks everywhere. One minute it was a burning building, the next, a smoldering pile of bricks. There were people screaming and crying, and I heard a siren in the distance. I felt my legs go out from under me, and I ended up sitting on the sidewalk just watching, slack-jawed.

The fire department got there and began cleaning things up. I was asked a few questions by the police as well, but everyone was more interested in helping those who'd just lost family or loved ones. For a moment, I saw things in sharp perspective: People hated me for reasons I couldn't control. But I had money in my pocket, and a roof over my head, and I was still alive. For the moment, that would have to do.

****

I got home about a half-hour later. Barney, my neighbor, was sitting on his stoop. He was one of the few people who seemed to harbor me no particular ill will. He gave me a little wave as I showed up.

"Hey Barney." I nodded. "Fire down on Bishop."

He winced. "Another one?"

I paused. "Another?"

He nodded. "You don't read the paper anymore?"

I chided myself. "Sorry, Barney, I've been... kinda distracted lately."

"Three fires, counting yours, in the past twenty-four hours. They said that zombi arsonist got caught before...

Maybe they were wrong?"

I'd never felt so bad having a suspicion confirmed. Still, I nodded and said, "Maybe."

Barney shrugged. "But enough of the bad stuff. How was work? Still getting chummy with the BNA?"

I really didn't want to talk about the Bureau. "Big contract today. Left me forty dollars."

Barney whistled appreciatively. "So you're buying dinner tonight, then?"

I smiled, a sensation recently unfamiliar to me. "I guess so."

****

The good times, Barney's company notwithstanding, were never long for my world. The next morning I woke up generally hung over and overheated; my fan had burned out while I slept. I walked to my office, and this time the bag of rats had been upgraded to some unidentifiable sticky substance that had been hurled at my window. It didn't take the glares of those who passed me on the street to drive home the fact that the public was making its displeasure known.

But I was already in a bad mood. When I saw the slop on my door, I turned and caught two women walking down the street who'd paused for just a moment to look at me. I narrowed my eyes at them. "What? This is my office. You want to come inside?"

They turned and moved quickly, and I called after them, "No one's driving me out of here, you get me? Nobody!"

It was angry, bitter, and pointless. The perfect start to the day.

The last infidelity job I had threw me into no end of hot water, so I decided to play this one a little more cautiously. An hour later I made up some story about taking the census as I rang the bell on Miss McDaniels' cracker-box-tiny home. My creativity came to no appreciable use, however, as there was no answer from within.

I went around back, and, after checking to be sure I wasn't observed, found the back door lock easily pickable. Once inside, I shut the door and re-locked it behind me.

The house was a small one, and neat as a pin, which was both good and bad. It meant I had to be careful to leave everything undisturbed, but it also meant that anything out of the ordinary would likely stick out.

In this case it was the tiny box under the bed. It had a small lock that took only a moment to bypass. Inside were pictures of Waldo, although nothing out of the ordinary. There were also letters, mostly from Waldo, but a few unsigned as well, that made my ears turn a bit red. If this Beverly was half as racy as the letters implied, I could see why Waldo was a little worried. I wasn't even involved with Beverly, and I was feeling a little uncomfortable myself.

I put everything back where I found it, and let myself out of the place. A quick talk with one of the neighbors under the guise of being in the neighborhood to read gas meters let me know that, yes, she'd seen Beverly and Waldo together. No, she hadn't seen them together recently. Yes, she'd seen Beverly that morning, and that she'd mentioned heading for the Andaris Observatory to meet a friend.

Never had I a lead so clear. I began to believe in luck as I walked the mile or two out to the observatory. It was even nice to be anonymous; no one was looking at me with the evil eye. It was pleasant. I knew it couldn't last.

I got to the park by the observatory and wandered a bit. Down by the nearby duck pond, I saw a couple eating a picnic lunch. A little shiver ran down my spine as I scanned the park. This is where I'd taken the picture that had lead me onto the trail of the necromancer who had given me such fame and infamy. I didn't like coincidences, nor did I trust them.

Another couple crossed the lawn as I made camp inside some tree cover. I steadied my nerves and took out the old camera, adjusting the lens while keeping an eye on the pair.

The girl was Beverly all right. I couldn't place the other guy, but that didn't mean much. Despite the heat, he wore a deerstalker cap that kept concealing his features. Of course I couldn't be lucky on that one.

The lunch meant little, though; it could easily be a cousin from back on the farm, or a colleague. I snapped a few shots, just in case.

When the couple packed up their lunch I put the camera away, and immediately regretted it. The kiss Beverly gave her companion was not the type given to one's cousin. Waldo had been right. And that meant I'd have to get more pictures. They always want pictures.

Beverly and her paramour hopped a cab, and I flagged another one down. It took a chunk of my pocket money to get him to agree to simply "follow that cab," and that combined with making sure I had plenty of film got filed away in the rapidly-growing expense report in my head.

The cab we were following headed into the Necropolis, and my cabbie muttered something disparaging under his breath. I'll admit, I don't live in the best neighborhood, which made this all the more strange. I began to wonder why Beverly would pick a place so out-of-the-way, and so out of her normal economic stature.

My blood chilled a little as the cab left the pair off at Walter and Vine. The no-questions-asked hotel on that corner had also been the central bit of set dressing on my last case of this nature. That case had ended with three murders, two bullet wounds on yours truly, and me making an enemy of the most powerful man in the city. Before I could ditch the whole thing, I reminded myself that a case was a case, and really, what more could fate do to me?

Remind me never again to pose that question.

I paid the cabbie and waited a minute or two, then headed inside. The desk clerk was someone new. I sauntered over and began inquiring about the couple who just came in.

Surprisingly, even a few dollars wouldn't get him to open up. "Oh no," he said, rapidly shaking his head side-to-side, "The last guy got fired for giving out information about the customers. No no no."

I frowned. Finding out which room Beverly and her beau were in would be essential. Finally, I reached into my pocket and pulled out my billfold. Money was usually the key for this, but in this case, I wasn't above a little misdirection.

"It's important," I said, holding up a business card, "And I'm in a hurry. You don't want to delay me."

The man looked at the embossed print from the BNA, and began to nod. My aggressive manner had kept the man from thinking that perhaps a real agent would show a badge, not a business card. He fumbled the register over to me, and I checked the most recent entry. Mister and Missus

Pate, room 206. Right next door to the room from the last case. My distrust in coincidences was starting to elevate to record levels.

It was a quick trip up the back fire escape to find the room and prep the camera. The blinds, much like the previous time, were damaged enough to see through and take pictures. Something was naggingly not right there. Still, the job had to be done; I'd been paid, and the expense account could use the boost. I also wasn't inundated with other offers.

The couple left the lights off, and thus I only saw silhouettes. They moved from embrace to kiss to bed rather quickly, and to say that they were both athletic and enthusiastic would be an understatement. They were loud, too. I began to realize why they wanted somewhere out of the way. No names were given in the throes of passion, but there was all manner of encouragement and entreaties. It sounded as if the racy letters at Beverly's home didn't exaggerate one little bit.

I got half a dozen photos, and I'll admit I felt a little sympathy for Waldo. No one likes the idea of infidelity, and they like it even less when they have to pay for the privilege of having it revealed to them in black and white.

When all was said and done, I crept back down the fire escape and strolled back to the office. It was just before closing time, but I decided to stick around and develop the pictures anyway. Just as I'd turned the office into an impromptu darkroom, the phone rang. I picked it up, and there was a short click before a nasal voice came over the line.

"This is the office of the Chicago branch of the Bureau of Necromantic Affairs. Is this Marcus Sage?"

"No, this is Grigori Rasputin."

There was a brief pause. I sighed as I remembered that everyone in the BNA had their sense of humor surgically removed. "Sorry, no, this is Marcus Sage."

"Mister Sage, Director Brody wishes to see you in his office at 9 AM tomorrow morning."

"That's nice. It sounds a little difficult, though, as I don't intend on being there."

"A car will be sent to your place of residence."

It was patently obvious that I wasn't being listened to, so I gave a cheery, "Drop dead!" And hung up the phone.

A half-hour later I'd finished developing the salacious pictures; the process was slowed due to the recent purchase of a bottle of good scotch that, while it wouldn't go on the expense account as such, would still be padded in somehow. I then took one more look at the silhouettes, locked the pictures in my file cabinet, congratulated myself on a job well done, and stumbled home.

****

The next morning I was still hot and annoyed when the knock came at my door. I'd been finishing breakfast and, for half a moment, I wondered just who had decided to bother me before I could make it to the office. I opened my front door, bleary-eyed, and saw a young man standing in a crisply-tailored suit standing on the front step.

"Mister Sage? Agent Doring."

"Why are you here?"

"Didn't you receive a phone call at your office last night?"

"No," I lied. "What's this about?"

Doring had the good grace to look a little sheepish. "Director Brody wants you at the office, post-haste."

"Ah, I see! Sorry, didn't realize. Come in."

I stepped back and didn't give Doring a moment to beg off from following me.

"I was just finishing breakfast. Let me go grab a cleaner shirt. I won't be a minute."

I could see Doring looking exceedingly uncomfortable about the whole process. I called back, "Is this about that thing?"

Doring either didn't know what this was about, or he was smart enough to realize I was fishing for information. "I'm afraid I can't say, Mister Sage."

I tied my tie as I passed him out the door, "Well, let's not keep the director waiting." Doring gave a half-smile that turned aghast as I added, "I haven't got all day to sit at the beck and call of that windbag."

Despite Doring's sudden distaste for me, we sped through Chicago traffic at a breakneck pace. Doring was good, and slid back and forth through the cars like a fish in a river. Finally, we parked less than a block from the building, and Doring gave me a stern gaze as we walked to the front door.

"Oh, there might be a problem," I noted off-handedly.

"What would that be?"

"The elevator's exclusive. I don't suppose you'll want to

walk up the stairs with me."

He narrowed his eyes. "You're an asset. You'll be allowed up."

"Oh gosh, sir, will I? I'm ever so grateful," I said, wide-eyed. Doring pointedly ignored me.

But he was right. The elevator operator apparently already recognized me, and showed only the tiniest amount of distaste at a black man being allowed in his domain.

We sped up to the fourth floor, and Doring led me to the door of Brody's office, where, after a brief knock, he ushered me in and shut the door behind me.

I'd been in Brody's office before. It was plush and well-appointed, and be it on the wall that held his diplomas, or the desk that held awards for his work across the nation smashing the necromantic threat, it was full of reminders that people like him, those who played ball with the powers that be, would get ahead, while people like me would have to scramble for every crumb we could grab.

Brody was on his phone, and motioned me in. I sat across from him, noting how even the chair seemed like more than I could afford with a month of good cases.

Finally, Brody hung up. "Marcus. Good to see you."

"I was summoned," I said, immediately realizing it sounded less friendly than it should have. I quickly added, "Sorry, had to deal with the elevator."

It took a moment for the penny to drop, and, to his credit, Brody looked appropriately sheepish.

"Sorry about that. You ready to get some work done?"

"No."

There was a long pause. He expected more banter. Finally, I decided to give it to him.

"Unless you're willing to pay my detective rates?"

His eyes narrowed. "You're playing ball with the BNA now, Sage."

"Does that mean I get paid agent rates?"

"You're... technically... not an agent until you do some paperwork--"

"--Which I'm not inclined to do."

The eyes narrowed further. "Maybe you'll change your mind once you've sobered up."

"There's always that possibility. I could also sprout wings and fly."

Brody had had enough. "Okay, fine. I want you to ride with two of my agents today. Rex and Beauford. They've been in for a couple of months from the Louisiana office, and could use a local."

I blinked. "That all?"

He sighed. "Yes. That's all. And once you've figured out on which side your bread is buttered, maybe you and I can have an actual discussion about your future, Sage."

"I'd be ever-so-grateful."

My sarcasm was obviously evident as Brody just stared at me angrily for a moment. He then picked up his phone and said to me, "Get out. Rex and Beauford will meet you at the elevator. Come back when you're thinking more clearly."

True to his word, there were a pair of agents waiting for

me by the elevator. Rex looked like he walked out of a fashion magazine; all suavity and hair tonic, and a grin so false you'd think he was getting ready for Halloween early. Beauford was six foot six of muscle straining inside an off-the-rack suit, and he radiated "good old boy," though with none of the "good" that might imply.

"You the new guy?"

Beauford's drawl set a twitch up my spine, but I'd be damned if I let him see that.

"Yeah, that's me."

There was no handshake offered from either side. Rex turned his grin up a notch.

"C'mon, spook. Let's hit the car park and you can play navigator."

I could tell right away exactly how enjoyable this was going to be.

After getting practically frog-marched out of the building along with the two agents, I was led out to a parking lot penned in by various tall buildings; the sort of place I'd never have noticed if I'd not been lead there. The BNA puts a premium on secrecy. It looked like that extended even into their cars.

Rex and Beauford walked quickly to one of the many identical black sedans with me trailing in their wake. Rex tossed his cigarette and slid into the driver's seat. Beauford paused for just a moment, looking at me, as if reminding me of my place in his world: The back seat was mine.

We drove around for about twenty minutes in complete silence. So much for navigation. I wanted to know where we were going, but I wasn't about to give Heckle and Jeckle the satisfaction of my ignorance. Finally, after circling a block twice, we parked in front of a brownstone in an upper-class neighborhood.

Rex and Beauford slid out of the car, and walked with authority. I followed. Again, to them, it was as if I didn't even exist. The three of us walked up the steps, and Beauford looked aside as Rex quickly took picks to the locks. A kid was passing by, and Beauford gave him a stare that sent him on his way. This was the way they worked, as if they didn't care who saw them. The people in the city were beneath them.

"Mind telling me what we're doing here?" I asked, the first words I'd said to the pair that entire day.

"Searching and interviewing."

"And you need to pick the lock for that?"

"Shut your mouth, spade," Beauford said, and Rex held up a hand to silence his partner.

"We prefer to make an entrance. Makes the subject less recalcitrant to speak. Watch and learn."

He stood and stepped back, and Beauford went for his gun. I immediately started to reach for mine, but Rex's grin made me realize this was all a game to them.

Beauford kicked open the door and yelled, "BNA. Make yourself seen, Joseph."

There was a bit of a scrambling noise from a back room, and a weak, tired voice said, "Wait! Just a minute!"

"Now!" Rex barked, and clicked back the hammer on his pistol. "Don't make me come back there."

It was only a moment later that Joseph walked out, his hands raised. Joseph looked to be about sixty years old, and sick. His hair was in clumps, and his skin was sallow and drawn. Unless the old man had something hidden in the pajamas and slippers he was wearing, Rex's gun was pure intimidation overkill.

"Sit down," Rex barked again, and Joseph, nodding, found a chair to drop his weary body into.

Beauford flipped out a notebook. "Joseph Kreigman."

The old man nodded as Beauford continued.

"Formerly lieutenant of the German 22nd infantry."

"You know that's me."

"Acquainted with the Nazi known as 'Nachtlowen'"

"How many times do I tell you? I don't know him, I never met him, the only time I hear his name is from you guys! I'm a good American now!"

Rex had slipped his pistol back into his shoulder holster, but he suddenly hauled off and punched the old man in the face with a blow that would've made my teeth rattle.

"You don't get to say that, Fritz. You don't ever get to say that."

Joseph had been knocked out of his chair, and I saw blood dripping from his mouth. He whimpered quietly, "Ja, I'm sorry... I'm sorry..."

Beauford looked completely nonchalant, "I'll put that down as a 'no.' You will tell us if he gets in touch with you?"

Joseph remained staring at the floor, but he nodded.

"We'll be back next week," Beauford said, "I suggest you have some sort of information for us." He then looked to me, "Any questions?"

I shook my head and tried to keep my rage in check. Beauford closed his notebook, and he and Rex made for the door. As I began to reach to help Joseph up, Rex barked, "C'mon, we haven't got all day."

I'd make them wait. I offered Joseph my hand, and he took it. As I raised him up, the sleeve of his pajamas slid up his arm, and I saw the crossed blackbirds tattooed on his forearm; the mark of those who'd been involved in the Nazi occult experiments that had brought necromancy onto the earth.

"Just go," he said quietly. "Just go."

I nodded to him and walked out, shutting the door behind me. Beauford looked at me critically. "Don't help the suspects. It's bad practice."

"What the hell was that all about?" I asked. "Beating down a defenseless man who you must've known didn't have the information you wanted?"

Rex shook his head as he walked toward the car. "He's sold a lot of necros up the river before. Besides, he was a Nazi, spade. An enemy of everything American."

As he wrenched open the door, he added, "Starting to wonder where your loyalties lie ...."

****

We drove in silence for a few miles, then Rex pulled the car over. I followed the pair as they walked to another brownstone. Rex pushed the door in, and I realized it had been ajar as we walked in. There was a scent here, much like the undead, and a touch of the cordite smell from a recently-fired gun.

Beauford decided to throw me a bone on this one. "Undead violence. The guy who lived here was on our watch list. Gunshots this morning."

"Someone called you?"

"Yeah. The goddamn chief of this precinct called us. He knows his job. Kreigman sold us this guy a couple of weeks ago, and now there's violence. Stupid fucking ghouls."

The last he'd said while looking directly at me, trying to get a reaction. I decided not to give him one. We walked into the kitchen. There was a younger-looking ghoul in a house dress, slumped over next to the kitchen table. Her face was a bloody mess about two inches away from a bowl of cereal that had fallen to the floor.

Rex gave me a slight grin. "Okay, I'll give you points for that one. Most people gag when they see stuff like this."

"I'm no amateur."

"So we hear." Beauford said. "So, you're a detective. Detect. Show us what you know."

I knelt near the body and checked the hands. Then the cereal and her dress. Then I paced the kitchen a few times, checking angles where she might've been shot from.

I was completely absorbed in the whys and wherefores of what had happened, and after mulling it all over in silence, I asked, "So who is she?"

No reply.

For a minute, I'd thought these guys were starting to show a little respect for my techniques. I could've told them that she'd just started up the stove when it happened. I could've told them she had only been half-dressed, and that whoever shot her liked her enough that he made sure the corpse wasn't naked. I could've told them all these things and more if they'd been sticking with me. But they hadn't. I turned and realized they'd just given me this crap to keep me busy while they went upstairs. Quietly, I followed, and I could hear the pair searching a nearby room.

"Look here."

A low whistle followed. "Looks like two hundred bucks."

"Nice."

"Hey, I get half of that."

"What about the spook?"

"Are you kidding?"

Rex laughed. "Yeah. Let's have him be a 'detective'. Maybe have him canvas the neighborhood."

"Like someone here's gonna talk to a spook from the squad?"

"Keeps him busy."

"Right."

I could hear the floor creak. They were coming my way. I was more right than I knew. I wasn't part of the BNA at all, and I certainly didn't want to be.

I didn't want to overplay my hand and let them know what had happened. I gave them a nice act, regurgitating all I'd found about the dead woman, and trying very gently to pump some information out of the pair. While I knew they hadn't caught on to me catching on, they were good; I wasn't able to get a thing out of them.

They did make me canvas the neighborhood while they no-doubt turned the place over for more loot, and when I got back, I'd practically solved what was an amazingly straight-forward case. The guy who owned the brownstone, Omar Reese, had a long-standing ghoul girlfriend, and that morning the two had been arguing. Then a gunshot. Rex and Beauford metaphorically patted me on the head like a dim child who'd just managed to squeak by on a math test, and we took off from there.

I took a break from Heckle and Jeckle when they so graciously went to a lunch counter that didn't serve anyone of my skin tone. They seemed to want to be rid of me as much as I wanted to be rid of them; I likely wasn't going to get into trouble for playing hooky, so I hopped a bus and headed back home. A night of oppressive heat followed. It felt like an entire day wasted.

****

The next day I was back in the office, and accomplished just as much as the day before, but at least I didn't have to deal with Mutt and Jeff. Before closing up shop, I gave Billings a call.

"Is Beverly... Is she..." There was something oddly expectant in his voice.

"I think we should talk about this face-to-face." Not only would it save time getting him the photos, but it would allow me to give my expense report as well.

"Very well," Waldo said. "Are you free tonight?"

I was very much in favor of ending this as quickly as humanly possible. "Sure. We can meet here at the office if you like."

"Oh, no, I was thinking perhaps the Knickerbocker hotel? I'll make dining room reservations."

I arched an eyebrow. "Mister Billings, normally matters of this nature are best handled privately."

"I'm going to be there anyway," he said. His voice sounded oddly excited. "I just want this finished."

"There's also the matter that the Knickerbocker doesn't allow Negros into its dining room."

"I've made arrangements."

I should've known something was up. Still... "Okay. I can be there in about an hour."

"An hour would be fine, Mister Sage."

****

I put the report and the photos into an envelope, and hopped a bus and a cab (both already on the expense report) to the Knickerbocker, one of the classier hotels in the city.

I got some stares as I walked in. A well-dressed ghoul woman gave me a look that could freeze Lake Michigan, and started talking in hushed tones to her companion, who started off, no doubt to get security.

I was just at the entrance to the dining room when the summoned man came over and stood in front of me. "Excuse me, sir. I think you may be in the wrong hotel."

I looked around, as if confused. "No, this is the

Knickerbocker."

He leaned in a little closer, "No, sir. You're in the wrong hotel."

"No, this is definitely the Knickerbocker."

"Let me help find you some other place to stay."

He reached out and was just about to put his hand on my shoulder when a purposeful cough stopped him. He turned, and the maître-d' behind him whispered something in his ear. His eyes went wide for a moment, and then he nodded. "I'm sorry, sir. There was a misunderstanding." It looked as if he'd rather be swallowing glass than saying so, but he continued. "Your party is waiting." I could only wonder what type of pull Mister Billings had, and reminded myself that staying on his good side might lead to bigger and better things. I prepared myself to be smooth.

"This way, sir." The maître-d' escorted me into the sizable dining room, mostly full with a later-evening crowd. The Knickerbocker once had a reputation as one of Capone's brother's hang-outs, but since the war and the name change, I suspected the new clientele weren't used to nightly scandal, such as a black man entering their eatery.

I stumbled in my step for just a moment. There was Waldo, waving me over. Across from him sat Beverly. My estimation of the man suddenly dropped; he wasn't just hoping to humiliate his cheating fiancée, he wanted to do it in public. Still, I couldn't just turn around and leave. I'd come this far, and this was really the client's business, as much as I disliked him. I put on a brave face and strolled over.

"Mister Sage," Waldo said, "So good to see you. Please, have a seat! Did you have any trouble getting in?"

"None that wasn't smoothed over. I assume that was your doing?"

He nodded, "I have a decent amount of pull here. Been a regular since the war. Oh, this is my fiancée, Beverly. I believe you already know her?"

Beverly offered her hand, but her look was one of confusion. I took it gracefully, and tried to keep my expression blank as I said, "Beverly. Nice to meet you."

"Charmed, I'm sure," she said, then looked to Waldo with a "what is this all about?" expression.

"Well, dear," Waldo said, "Mister Sage has some photos to share with us. Don't you, Mister Sage?"

He'd raised his voice slightly, and now we had an audience of most of the nearby tables.

"Are you sure you don't want to handle this in private?"

"Most certain, Mister Sage." He was grinning now. I began to feel a little queasy. Mister Billings was more twisted than I'd anticipated. I didn't know I was only half-right.

I took out the folder and handed it to Waldo. As he took it, I held on a second longer and made eye contact. Quietly, I said, "These are… explicit. You probably don't want to show them off here."

"Nonsense." Waldo said, almost yanking the folder from my grasp. "Here, Beverly. What do you think of these?"

He flipped open the folder and spilled the photos out on the table. The top ones were from the park, but the lower, more carnal ones, splayed out over the table as well.

Beverly looked horrified. "Oh my!"

I suddenly realized that a few people from the nearby tables had actually gotten up and come over. Waldo was grinning like a Cheshire cat, and the man who'd come up behind him whistled low and murmured, "Nice."

"Yes, quite the infidelity!" said another.

I was a little too flabbergasted by Waldo's grin and general demeanor to react, but what really bowled me over was Beverly. Here were photos of her in flagrante with another man, and while her blush was red-hot, she was... smiling.

Another of the men patted her on the back, and a couple women were blushing as well, but only showing the barest hints of mock outrage.

"Thank you, Mister Sage," Waldo grinned, "What do I owe you for the expenses?"

You could've knocked me over with a feather. "What the hell is going on here?" I grumbled.

He laughed. "Oh, yes. Well. That man in the photos, that's me."

I looked more closely. It... might've been true. But he wasn't the...

I paused, looking at the park photos, then looking at him, then back at the photos. It was him. Him with make-up and a prosthetic nose and probably a wig.

"It's quite all right, you see? Just a little excitement for me and my friends."

"What?" The urge to punch him in the face was rising.

"Oh come on, Mister Sage. You've been in the papers!" Beverly said.

"And being trailed by the famous Negro private investigator into the heart of zombitown where her torrid affair was consummated? Brilliant!" Waldo grinned maniacally. "And quite fun, too!"

There was more back-slapping. I growled, "So this was all some sort of joke?"

"Oh, yes, Mister Sage." Waldo said. "I'm sorry we couldn't tell you, but you might not've played along! So, how much do I owe you?"

The punching urge kept rising, but luckily it never slipped past the level of me wanting to get paid.

"Another twenty-five in expenses."

It was five times what I'd actually accrued, but Waldo pulled out the bills and laid them on the table like they were nothing to him. They probably were.

And suddenly so was I. The friends Waldo and Beverly had brought over to witness the climax of their little lovers' game were engrossed in the photos and the details, and Waldo and Beverly looked so damn proud of themselves. When I took the bills and stormed off, I don't think anyone even noticed.

****

I'm a lot of things to a lot of people, and for money I can be even more, but I'm not a patsy to any man, no matter how thick his wallet is. The people at the Knickerbocker weren't sad to see me go, and the doorman ignored me when I asked him to hail me a cab, so it came down to me calling one up from a local payphone.

A half-hour later I was back in the Necropolis. I got dropped off at home, but after some thought as to the money I had in my pocket, and my need to either get staggeringly drunk or thrash someone twice my size (or perhaps both), I decided to take a walk over to the Blackpoole.

For those of you who haven't followed my little tales of woe up until this point, the Blackpoole is one of the most notorious clubs in the city. The place has hot bands and plenty of readily-flowing

booze at any point of the quality spectrum six nights a week. There are loud rumors that it caters to Renfields; it's a hot meet-up spot for the living and the unliving to dance their cares away with each other, and perhaps go further than that when the night ends. I won't confirm nor deny those rumors. I don't get paid to.

The star of the attraction is Mamu Waldi. She owns the Blackpoole, and she's got her finger on the pulse of almost every shadowy event that happens in our dark corner of the globe. She's a ruthless businesswoman, smart as a whip, and has legs that go on to eternity. She also used a strange knife to slash the throats of two men in front of me in her club not too long ago. Granted, the men were trying to kill us at the time, but I woke up in cold sweats for a few days after that incident. Still, she'd saved our lives, and that meant something.

A building a few doors down from the 'poole had been the target of the zombi arson when it started a good month ago. While the clean-up had continued, the Blackpoole had been covered in ash. I suspect that Mamu looked at this as a happy decorating accident, and thus the street around the club was still black and sooty. People stood in line to get into the club most nights, and their shoes would track the darkness into the building.

At that moment, however, there were only one or two people outside, chatting with each other. I could hear the music and the crowd, and figured I was back amongst friends, or, at the very least, a whiskey bottle that would substitute for a friend.

Fred and Marvin, a double-act of a well-dressed zombi and an equally dapper ghoul, kept watch on the front door. They'd helped Mamu repel the invaders who had threatened their boss and tried to end my life, and that made them all right in my book. Besides, Marvin had more of a sense of humor than most ghouls I knew: Gallows humor, to be sure, but a sense of humor none the less.

I strolled up, and Marvin held up a hand. "Sorry, Sage."

Figuring he was joking, I tried to brush past him. He didn't budge, and I felt Fred's cold hand on my shoulder.

"You're not allowed in."

"What the hell?" I shrugged Fred's hand off, but it returned quickly.

"Sorry. Boss's orders," Marvin replied. "You're not allowed in."

"Marvin, what the hell is going on? I know the last time I was here things got a little hectic, but I helped Mamu get out of that, remember?"

He shrugged. "It's not about that."

"What is it about then?"

He looked downward for a moment, then made eye contact again. "The BNA has already been here twice this week."

I felt the fury that had started to calm during my journey from the Knickerbocker start to rise again, and I wasn't even sure who it was aimed at: Billings, for playing me like a sap? Mamu, for blacklisting me? The BNA, for turning me into a pariah in my own local club? Marvin, for not letting me in? At that moment, my rage was focused on the ghoul-at-hand, but in the end, it's pointless to get furious at the undead. It's like throwing a stone into the ocean and hoping for a tidal wave. Marvin just looked at me blankly.

I gritted my teeth. For a moment, I just wanted to shove my fist in his face. Luckily, common sense prevailed. "Yeah. Well. Tell her to call me."

He nodded, and said no more. I stormed off back into the night.

****

It had been only a few days earlier that I had walked into Mamu's club, and into a nightmare.

I'll admit, I don't have the light step of a ballerina, but I'd somehow kicked over an anthill that included both one of the city's up-and-coming mob figures as well as a powerful gwambi. For those who don't know what a gwambi is, consider: If a necromancer is a pistol, a gwambi is an atom bomb. And the one I'd ticked off? Mamu had confirmed for me that he had to be a big one.

She was looking at me through lidded eyes in the main room of her club as we interrogated "big" Jonas Sexton, a man whose rise in the ranks of the underworld was predicated on his ability to strangle people both efficiently and ruthlessly.

"He's not going to talk, Sage." Her voice was like ice. She had reason for her shivering hatred; Sexton had, not minutes earlier, held her hostage in order to get to me. It was a mixture of quick thinking and dumb luck that had turned the tables, with a side-order of Marvin and Fred coming in as the cavalry.

Sexton looked up at me from his kneeling position on the floor, and it looked as if Mamu might be right; his glare showed the certain impertinence of one who believes in his own invulnerability.

I decided to cut that right off with a backhand, but he didn't budge. In fact, he laughed.

Mamu had been wielding a strange, dark-bladed knife when we'd fought our way through the goons. She took it out and played with it at the end of her fingertips. "Let me take the words out of him, Sage."

I shook my head, and was about to speak, but the knife slashed out. Sexton screamed. There was blood everywhere.

I looked to Mamu. "Dammit, he was my trump card!"

She looked at me, and her gaze was a mixture of predatory hunger and the pity said predator might feel for a dumb animal at the other end of the hunt. "The gwambi controlled him, and now he'll be after you, Sage. This blade is the only thing that can sever that link."

And with a movement as tender as a lover's caress, she slashed my throat.

I woke up under my bed. I couldn't move for a few moments. The nightmare had hit me like a train. My entire body was tense to the point of pain.

I had a bottle of scotch lying next to me, and another one by my feet. I had no recollection of how I'd gotten them, or how we all ended up under the bed. But there we were.

My hangover could kill an elephant, and I felt it through every single part of my body. God's own flashlight came blazing in from the window, as if the Almighty wanted to be sure I was getting up in time to greet the punishment for overindulgence. Somewhere in the distance, my phone rang. It sounded like an orchestra playing the 1812 Overture at point-blank range.

I dragged myself to the shower and let the water pound down on top of me. Slowly, the pain began to fade from my limbs. Unfortunately, as I began to focus, I started to get angry again. Angry at all of those around me changing their views over what and who I was. Angry at myself, too... But I wasn't ready to admit that just yet.

The muscle soreness was dissipating, but the headache wouldn't leave, and now it was being fueled by a deep sense of rage and resentment. I toweled myself off and considered not even heading for the office that day, when the phone began to ring again.

I picked up the receiver and barked into it. "What?"

The voice was a familiar one, last heard on my office line. "This is the office of the Chicago branch of the Bureau of Necromantic Affairs. Is this Marcus Sage?"

"Yes. But I'm tremendously hung over. Drop dead."

"Sober up quickly, Mister Sage. A car is coming to pick you up."

I slammed the phone down. I was in no mood for banter. I slumped into the chair by the phone, but after growling at the walls for a few minutes I got dressed, then collapsed back onto my bed.

After some few minutes, I heard a knocking at the door. A minute or so passed, and it repeated. Another minute, then a tapping at the window of the entryway. I began to realize that playing dead wasn't going to get me out of this; it'd just mean more percussive noise to batter my hangover, and more chance of the neighbors seeing a BNA agent on my front step, thus cementing my Benedict Arnold status.

I cursed softly and opened the door, finding the same young agent who had chauffeured me the day before. I glared at him. "I suppose telling you I'm hung over won't make a difference."

"No. I've been told to retrieve you, and that's what I plan on doing."

"You're a good little dog, aren't you?"

My attempts to pick a fight weren't working. He just stared at me, his look being one more of pity than of anger. "Get your tie and hat. You have three minutes."

I stumbled back inside, feeling like a child being chided for not being ready for church. All it did was serve to aggravate me further. I finished getting dressed, then pushed past the agent into the car.

During the drive, his feeling of disapproval was pretty much palpable. We sped through the streets of Chicago, and I swear he made a few extra sudden stops and starts, just to make me feel like I would eject my breakfast. The joke was on him. I hadn't eaten any.

As we pulled up to the BNA offices, Agent Doring looked over his shoulder, his look of mild disgust completely undisguised. "Do you want to take the stairs, or shall I escort you to the elevator?"

I made a noncommittal grunt, and followed the agent into the building, past security, and into the elevator. The initial jerk of the car once again made me feel like I was going to vomit, but we made it to Director Brody's office without incident. My chauffeur glared at me and ushered me inside, letting the door close a little too loudly behind me.

Brody was at his desk, and for once it looked like he'd expected to give me his complete attention.

"So, Marcus. Time for a debriefing."

I stumbled slightly as I got to the chair and sat down. Brody shook his head sadly. "I see there was alcohol on the menu last night. Likely as the main course?"

I grumbled an assent, and Brody took a bottle from his desk. "Hair of the dog?"

Again, I nodded, and a minute or two later I was postponing my headache till a later time. "Thanks," I said quietly, although I didn't mean it.

"You're welcome," he said, likely at the same level of sincerity. "Agents usually don't show up hung over."

"I'm not an agent. I'm an asset, remember? And I didn't have much choice."

He tsk'd, "You'd have more choice if you were an agent, you know. Now, tell me about the day."

"You sent me out to be babysat with two goons who roughed up some guy, then looted a crime scene. They're not new, like you said they were. Thanks for that."

Brody didn't show a single ounce of surprise or remorse. "You dislike this?"

"You're damn right I do! If you want to use me, put me on something worth my time!"

"I will when you show you're worth it. Dammit, Sage, you've fought this every step of the way, kicking and screaming like a petulant child."

The words stung, and I couldn't come up with a good retort. After a moment, Brody continued.

"You've got skills, Marcus. Good ones. And good instincts. But you and everyone else in the Necropolis looks at us as the enemy. We're fighting a rising tide of blood that's going to drown the city, and without eyes and ears in the Necropolis, we're half-blind."

"Find someone else."

"And leave you out so Tilman Andaris can get his hands on you? Let me tell you something, Sage. Already he's making moves to get you kicked out of here. My superiors want to play ball with him, so they want you out. There are people in this building who think it's a goddamn disgrace that a Negro could get a BNA badge, and they want you out, too. I know if you step foot out of here without our backing, Andaris will have you dead before sundown. *We* are protecting you from that! I know you have talents that you're wasting, and you could help us take the necros in the city out of the game. But before you can do that, you have to show you're willing to be a team player, Sage. Now straighten up and fly right, for chrissakes!"

I blinked. He was right, about all of it, but I was so angry I could scream. "I'm sorry. I wasn't listening. Could you repeat that?"

Brody stared daggers at me. "Get out of my office, Sage. Come back tomorrow when you're completely sober. I'm going to lie and say you're on assignment from me.

Tomorrow you're going to come in here and act like an adult, and we'll get this ironed out. Got me?"

I nodded somewhat dismissively. "Can I go now?"

"Go. Now." Brody's voice was like ice. He looked down at some papers on his desk, and at that point, in his mind, I wasn't even there.

I obliged him of that perspective, and left, taking the stairs down to the lobby and hailing a cab from there.

****

I ended up not going to the office. I was still hungover and mad, and I knew that getting drunk probably wasn't an option; or at least not a good one. I just wanted to take off the tie and coat and seethe quietly for a while.

I spent the better part of three hours just sitting in my house, listening to the radio. Music, a soap opera, then the news. Tilman Andaris was hosting a Halloween party for the city's upper crust. My invitation was no doubt lost in the mail.

After I began to cool down, and the world no longer sounded like a long-term assault on my ears, I opened the windows to let some air in.

Barney was sitting on his stoop, carving a jack-o-lantern. He gave me a nod and said, "You all right, Marcus?"

"Bad day," I said. I felt suddenly drained. Being angry robbed me of all my energy.

"You maybe want some dinner tonight? My nephew

Reggie was over earlier today, he brought some Chinese take-out from where he works. You can't say no to eggroll, can you?"

I chuckled. Even on the bad days, Barney had my back. I nodded. "So long as I don't have to get dressed up."

He waved it off. "We'll eat in front of the TV. Saddler's fighting tonight from New York. Don't want to miss that!"

"Fine, fine. I don't need more of the hard sell."

"Hey, it just looks like you could use a night off. Tell you what, we'll watch, you can vent about the BNA, and you can even carve one of the other pumpkins if you like."

"Barney, you're a scholar and a gentleman."

"And my intelligence is only exceeded by my good looks!" he insisted.

I chuckled again. "Let me get cleaned up. I'll be over in about a half-hour."

****

A half hour later, and we were feasting on leftover Chinese food and waiting for the fights to come on. I gave the whole sad tale of my morning, and Barney commiserated. The news blathered on about the continued diplomatic problems between the US and Russia. I was pretty sure Barney had come from Europe, and he just shook his head sadly, "We can't get along, even when there's not a war. What sort of world are we leaving the kids? I swear, some days I think it should just all burn."

A brief story came on about a major warehouse fire in

New York, and how a pair of zombis were to blame. Barney once again bemoaned this, but I wasn't listening. Another arson, by zombis? When they'd been happening in the city, I had learned the whole thing might've been a side effect of a mass zombification process. Was something like that happening elsewhere? For a moment, I debated whether I should tell Brody so he could tell his superiors. I rankled at the idea. I'd be showing him that I was a "team player" and largely his underling. Let him find his own facts.

The next morning I knew I was supposed to report back to Brody, but I really wasn't of a mind to. When the phone call came, I politely ignored it. When the phone began to ring again, I realized that either the calls would keep coming, or a car would come and the driver would wait for me. I decided that playing hooky was my best option.

I ended up heading over to the gardens on Twelfth. The day was hot and windy, and I got to watch people feed ducks and sail tiny boats around the man-made lagoon. It wasn't bad, really. I didn't have to watch anyone suspiciously, I didn't have to follow anyone, I didn't have to worry that the ghoul with the easel and paints watching the children play wasn't actually some assassin after me. All in all, it was a perfectly relaxing day. Or it would've been, had the nagging fact not come to mind that the money I had from Billings would run out sooner or later, and that I'd have to do something to pay for this lavish lifestyle I was leading.

I've never been a guy who likes to sit idle, and the guilt over such a situation started to sink in as the sun started setting and people started heading back home. I began to walk, a little aimlessly. It was time to do some thinking about the future. Brody had saved my life, three times. Granted, I'd paid him back by saving his life twice, but still... Would it be that bad to work for him? On the other hand, the BNA seemed to take an almost gleeful pleasure in stomping all over my neighborhood, and it was eminently clear that I wasn't about to be able to change that from the inside. It seemed like no one trusted me locally anymore, and that reputation was going to make it harder and harder to get work to come my way, not to mention the ability to get people to cooperate with my investigations. And then there was Mamu. I didn't even want to think about her. It wasn't just the fact that her displeasure could ruin anyone in town; Mamu and I had been, I thought, the closest thing to friends that people in our respective lines of work could hope to be. I wondered if I'd misinterpreted where we stood with each other.

I'd left the apartments and brownstones of the residential district, and wandered into the warehouse district. The buildings here used to be full at all times, providing for the war effort. Since then, many of them had become empty shells, abandoned hulks along the waterfront. One of them had become a drop point for me when I needed to hide things outside the office. I took in the atmosphere, realized I wasn't even close to solving the world's problems, much less my own, and decided to head back home.

I began heading in that direction when I heard an odd noise. It was a half-chuckle, half whistle; like someone trying to laugh with a case of pneumonia. I heard it again, from inside the warehouse whose loading doors I was standing beside.

Something seemed familiar about the noise, and I decided to give it a look. I tried the loading door with no luck, and then headed around back. The door there was wide open; it looked like it might've been pried with a crowbar. The hairs on the back of my neck weren't just standing up at that point; they were practically saluting.

I crept in with my pistol drawn. The noise was coming from somewhere beyond the stacks of palettes and old crates. It came again, and something nagged at the back of my mind. Something I couldn't quite place.

A sharp, acrid scent wafted to me, and I barely held myself back from sneezing. I could hear the noise coming from just beyond a stack of crates ahead of me. I'd either need to backtrack or climb. I chose the latter.

I was just atop the crates when I started smelling the smoke.

The blast from the chemical fumes wasn't huge, but it was enough to knock the stack of crates down and snatch the wind from my lungs. I was pinned under a bunch of wood, some of it on fire, and I could barely breathe.

Desperately, I began to push the fallen wood, twisting my leg to get it free. I could hear that cackle-whistle moving away slowly, and I heard the crackle of another set of crates going up.

I struggled loose, and managed to have only my foot stuck under the broken crates, when the owner of the strange noise and the firebug tendencies came back around a stack of palettes.

It was Fred.

My eyes went wide. He was cackling and dragging a can of kerosene, pouring what little was left in it over the palettes, then taking out a match.

"Fred? What the hell is going on?"

He ignored me, and I kept pulling and pushing to get myself free. "Fred! Get over here and help me!"

For a moment, he stopped the whistle-cackle, and

looked directly at me. His expression, for the briefest of instances, was one of horror and pain. I'd never seen him show emotion before.

He took one step toward me, then froze, and walked back beyond the next stack of crates. I could hear breaking and smashing.

The fire was jumping from crate to palette, and climbing up the walls. The smoke was getting thick and began burning my lungs. I finally got my foot free, and debated only for a moment the idea of running out of the place. It was a non-starter; I had to know what the hell was going on, and I'd be damned if I'd let Fred burn.

I ran through the burning warehouse, trying to pick out the sound of Fred's whistle-laugh over the crackle and roar of the flames. I ended up dodging and barely avoiding a collapsing pillar that scorched my coat sleeve. The heat was becoming unbearable, but there was no way I was going to let this slip through my fingers.

Finally, ahead, I saw Fred. He was trying to light a match, but seemed to be stymied by the process. I called his name once again, and he turned, but the look on his face was no longer anything but pure hate and malice.

"We're getting out of here, Fred. I don't know what happened to you, but we need to get out before the whole place comes down!"

I stepped forward and Fred backhanded me.

The strength of a zombi is a prodigious thing, and I was slammed to the ground. Luckily, he seemed too obsessed with getting the match lit to follow up on the damage.

Staggering to my feet, and trying to catch my breath, I leaped on Fred's back and tried to get control of his arms.

He tossed me off like I was an old overcoat, and I rolled to barely avoid a small flaming pool on the floor. I wasn't fully successful; the sleeve of my coat caught fire.

I began ripping it off, but I then noticed Fred turn and stare at me. I held up the burning coat. His eyes followed it. His addled mind had found a replacement for his match.

I held it out toward him, and he reached. Luckily, while Fred was probably ten times as strong as me, he wasn't very quick. I backpedaled, and he followed.

My breath was coming in gasps, and I was wheezing through smoke and chemical fumes as I backed across the burning warehouse, keeping Fred in my sights. I knew once I got him out, it would take somehow talking to Mamu to figure out Fred's motivation; it's not like he'd be able to tell me.

For a moment, however, I thought. I never knew where Mamu got her zombis. We joked about it from time to time, but she never told me. The first arson was right near the Blackpoole. Mamu had a strong aversion (to put it mildly) to having the BNA even inside her club...

My thought process was interrupted as a stack of burning crates collapsed just behind me. My way out was blocked. Fred was coming for my jacket, which was blazing like a torch at the end of my hand. I had to think fast.

There was a small gap between the crates to my right. The stack was on fire, but I could see the front door, ajar, not that far beyond them.

I had little choice. I wedged myself between the crates and continued to hold out the jacket to bring Fred along. He was narrow, like most zombis; he'd be able to fit through if I could.

I was half way through when something above me gave way, and the stacks of crates leaned against each other. I could feel the fire licking against my back, searing my skin. I was wedged in, and I began to panic. The crates above me were coming apart, and would soon drop a few hundred pounds of burning wood atop my head. I flailed and twisted hopelessly.

Suddenly, I felt an almighty force slam against my left shoulder. I skidded out from between the crates, and as I gained my feet at the front door, I got one last look at Fred. He'd pushed me. No matter what had happened to him, he found the wherewithal to save my life.

It was my last look. The crates, and a moment after, the entire ceiling, collapsed in flame on top of the zombi who'd just saved my life.

****

I awoke in the hospital the next day. I'd been found wandering around the area in a daze by the fire department. Second-degree burns on my back and arm needed to be treated, as well as minor smoke inhalation. I was in and out of consciousness from the pain for most of the day, and thus the BNA gave me enough leeway that they didn't send agents to interrogate me until late the next evening.

I'd considered telling them to buzz off, but now I had as many questions as answers, and figured it might be worth my while to go a little quid-pro-quo on them. I told them everything I'd witnessed in the warehouse, and that I'd remembered afterward that the whistle-laugh might've been what I'd heard when I first encountered a zombi arsonist about a week previous. In return, I tried to get from them whether the Bureau figured this was in some way connected to the fire in New York, and whether they found anything out from the dismantling of the mass-zombi-production warehouse a few days after that.

What I learned is that the BNA agents were decidedly all take and no give. After some stonewalling, they at least agreed to bring my concerns to Director Brody.

The next day, much to my surprise, Brody himself showed up. He even brought me a card, which I felt was gilding the lily a tiny bit. He went over the exact same information that his agents had gone through, but after confirming everything I'd already told them, he was actually willing to discuss some of my pet theories and questions with me.

"The New York incident is something that's being sent back and forth between offices at the moment. There may well be a connection."

"You think someone is doing a mass-production in New York?"

"We're looking for patterns ..." He hesitated for a moment, then shook his head.

"What?"

"You know I shouldn't be sharing any of this with you. There's a lot of confidential information here."

"What about the whistling?"

"Confidential."

"Oh come on, Brody! It's obviously important, can you at least tell me why I've run into two pyromaniac zombis who both have the same odd speech-and-music predilection?"

"Nice word. You get a thesaurus for your birthday?"

"Brody!"

I winced as I think I pulled a stitch somewhere. Brody frowned. "I'm not going to give you the hard sell. But if you were with us..."

"Don't give me that, Brody!"

He paused, and leaned back in his chair, "You want answers? Fine. Go talk to that witch who lives in the Necro."

"Mamu?"

"She won't talk to any of us. And you said yourself you thought she was involved in this. The zombi was hers. Once that gets out, it's for the law."

"She'd rather drive a stake through my heart than talk to me right now."

"Really? File says you're quite close."

"You have a file on her?" It was a stupid question.

"And on you, champ. We watch everybody. We keep the shadows at bay."

"Yeah, you're doing a bang-up job of that."

He stood and put on his hat. "If you want answers and you don't want to sign on, she's your best shot. Go work that legendary Sage charm on her. Barring that, let her know that once the ashes settle at that warehouse, we're going to come calling personally for this one, and her minions won't be keeping us out."

He left, and I shuddered. If the BNA and Mamu clashed, the Necropolis would be right in the middle, and that could easily be more explosive than any arsonist's fever dream.

****

It was October 30th when I got out of the hospital. I caught a cab back home and spent a good chunk of the morning getting clean and rested. I phoned the Blackpoole. No answer in Mamu's office or at the bar.

I dressed as sharply as I could and took the walk down to the club. From a distance, it looked as silent as the grave. The door was locked tight, and, of course, Fred wasn't there.

After a lack of response to my knocking, I found a neighborhood kid playing hopscotch on the sidewalk. I paid him a dime, and he let me know that Mamu and her employees were at Lazarus Hill. He then called me a fed rat and ran after I turned my back.

Lazarus Hill was the popular location for the twice-dead to be laid to rest. They were going to have a funeral for Fred. It made sense, and I felt like a bit of a heel for not thinking about it in the first place.

I caught a cab with my dwindling roll of bills, and walked into the graveyard just as a hard, cold breeze blasted by me. My shiver, however, had little to do with that.

There was a tiny gathering by the graveside. Marvin was there, as was Wickes, the bartender. A couple other people, two of them zombis, were giving each other sad looks. A man in a black suit and tie spoke to the gathered of faith for the end-times.

Of course, on the edge of it all was Mamu. She wore a black veil, and a tasteful black dress. She was crying. I think it was the only time I'd ever seen her like that, and it made something inside me hurt.

Marvin was standing next to Mamu, and when he looked up and saw me, he whispered to her. She looked my way, and even from my distance, I could sense her distaste. I decided to keep my distance.

The service ended, and the body was buried. A few mourners stayed as the earth was shoveled on top of the coffin. Mamu said something to Marvin, then made a beeline for me.

I'd planned all sorts of questions, but they all vanished when she slapped me, hard. I held my jaw. "I suppose I deserve that."

"And so much more," she hissed.

I could only nod. Not all of this was my fault, but enough of her problems all came home to roost when I was around. I could understand her hatred.

She leaned in, and for a moment, it was almost as if we were close again. The tone of her voice, however, dispelled that notion.

"Find who did this to Fred," she said, her voice barely above a whisper, "Find him and put him in the ground."

It was a natural request. The kind one would make to family in this twisted, tainted corner of the city we lived in.

I only struggled with my answer for a moment.

"I will."

"Once you do that, we're good again, Sage. We're good again."

Something in my gut sank. I was selling my soul to be in her good books again. But this would be justice, wouldn't it?

I nodded. "I'll get the guy."

"I know you will."

She touched my hand for a moment, then walked back to the rest of the mourners. Marvin looked my way, and gave me a nod. It was, perhaps, the most emotional moment he and I had ever shared.

****

Marvin was good enough to come to my office to talk about what had happened. It was a cheap trick, but even if I could've gotten into the Blackpoole, I liked having the home-ground advantage.

"Someone left a bag of rats on your doorstep," Marvin informed me.

I sighed. "It's a wonder they have any left to give me at this point."

Marvin sat. "It's also a shame. I know why they're doing that, Mister Sage. And they shouldn't."

I arched an eyebrow. "You're going soft on me?"

He shook his head slowly, and his voice was as cold as the grave. "We have to stick together, Mister Sage. All of us. There's a darkness out there that wants nothing more than to make the entire world a charnel house. If we don't stay together, we're lost."

I looked at Marvin intently. "Are you talking about something in particular?"

His eyes seemed to go colder and more distant, if such a thing was possible. "It's something that I feel, just a little bit. That there's something out there that's pressing against this world. Something both dark and sinister."

"Did Fred feel that way?"

Marvin nodded. "He did. Even more so than I do."

I took out a bottle and poured myself a drink. I offered one over, but Marvin waved it off. After taking a long sip, I asked, "Did Fred have enemies?"

"Many. But we both did. We turned away a lot of people from the club. But I can't imagine any of them having the wherewithal to do this to someone."

"Do you think it was necromancy?"

He shrugged. "Maybe? Just because I'm dead doesn't mean I know how it all works."

"Yeah, sorry. Do you have any ideas, any theories why this might have happened?"

"No. Not really."

I sighed again. "Okay, let's start from the beginning. How long did you know Fred?"

"All my life."

"All your post-death existence?"

Marvin shook his head. "All my life. Fred was my brother."

It knocked the wind out of me. "I'm so sorry."

"Yeah, well," Marvin said, looking down at the desk. "We hadn't seen each other in years. He was in Germany before the war. I didn't see him until after..." He trailed off.

"He was already dead at that point?"

Marvin nodded. "I was the last of his family left. They shipped him here, cargo, like a lot of the other zombis. I... was just lucky to get my brother back. Some people weren't so fortunate."

I hesitated at the next question, but it had to be asked.

"So, he was ... probably part of the original program?"

"The Nazi programs? Maybe. There aren't really records. It might've been some rogue necromancer. I never found out. Almost all of Fred's memories were gone. He barely recognized me."

"I'm sorry."

Marvin waved it off. "Let's just find out what happened, okay?"

"Right. Then ... He stayed with you?"

"Or at the club. Mamu is... very good to us."

"He have other people he interacted with?"

"No, not really. Just the people at the club."

I tapped my pen lightly on the table. "All right. Maybe I can dig up something from the BNA that might help with this."

"They going to play ball with you?"

"I doubt it," I grumbled. "They don't like me much these days. But that doesn't mean I can't get the information."

Marvin nodded, "I suspect you're able, Mister Sage." He then hesitated for just a moment, before saying, "I know Mamu and you are on the outs right now, but understand...she's always said you were the most capable person she knew. That's why I suggested turning to you."

I was surprised. "You did that?"

He nodded. "It's as I said, Mister Sage. If we don't stay together, we are lost."

****

That afternoon, I snagged a stack of folders from the BNA under the lie that Director Brody had suggested I look them over. There'd be hell to pay for that, but at that moment, I'd been left scratching my head over Fred's death. Even if my contacts had deigned to speak with me, I wasn't sure any of them had the answers either. So, for once I was going to do what Brody had been pushing me to do since the day the newspapers made me a de facto agent; I was going to use their resources like a good little fed.

The top folders were about the case I'd been working with Rex and Beauford. I'd used that as camouflage; everyone would assume that was what I should be looking at. I thumbed through the information on Omar Reese and his girlfriend whom I had examined, Sarah Gomert. Gomert had been reanimated by a necro who'd been put in prison some seven years ago. Omar's file was full of references to "File X27," and that particular one wasn't in my stack. I figured it was likely whatever Rex and Beauford had actually been looking for when they pocketed Omar's money. I didn't particularly care.

I was looking for anything that might connect Fred with the other arsons when I froze. The next file in the stack was Tilman Andaris'. Pandora's box, mine for the opening. A thick folder was below the case file, and it looked juicy with secrets. I flipped it open, grabbed the first stack of photographs and papers, and began reading.

Two hours later my smile was gone, and the papers were thrown haphazardly across my desk. I'd managed to get a nice knowledge of Andaris' early years; how he'd grown up locally, son of wealthy industrialist Efram Andaris. Private schools. Time in Europe. Then immediately back home after Pearl Harbor.

Thing is, that's where it ended. There was a memo tucked into the back of the folder, mentioning that any other information about Andaris was classified and would have to be directly requisitioned from the director of operations.

"Great," I grumbled, "Useless." Frustrated, I pushed the file off the desk.

Beneath it was the file on the other case Rex and Beauford had brought me to. Joseph Kreigman. I figured if I had the files out, I should seem like I'd done something with them, so I flipped that one open.

The first picture made my heart leap into my throat.

Joseph Kreigman was in a Nazi uniform. He was spit and polish, and looked nothing like the worn-out old man Rex had smashed in the face. He looked confident, and proud, with a half-grin. A half-grin I'd seen before. Kreigman had been at Dachau when the dead rose.

****

Despite the oppressive heat of the sun beating down on me, I felt as cold as ice the next morning as I took a bus to Joseph Kreigman's neighborhood. I watched the children running about in their Halloween costumes, but none of it could bring me joy. I was about to walk into a memory with hounds that I'd largely been able to keep at bay with significant levels of whiskey. This time, I wouldn't have that armor. I'd have to go in stone cold sober.

The knock on the door went unanswered. I thought about Rex picking it the day before, and hesitated only for a moment. The agents could get away with drawing a cold stare, but a black man picking the lock of an elderly white man's door in the early morning would get more than just unfriendly glances.

I walked around to the back alley behind the houses, and was rewarded for my caution by a back door with a lock that was as easy to circumvent as Rex had made the front door appear. Still, I didn't want to give the man a heart attack. I walked into his kitchen and called out, "Joseph Kreigman?"

No answer. I was about to call out again while walking into the living room, when I heard a low groan from upstairs.

I hustled upward. "Mister Kreigman?"

The moan came from the bedroom. I opened the door, and there was a nightmare I hadn't expected.

Kreigman had kept his uniform. Somehow he'd brought it into the states and, I suspect, no one had seen it. He'd kept it in good repair, and, were it not the symbol of the enemy that had brought the dead back from the grave, he'd have looked almost handsome in it.

He was laying on his bed, moving only a little, his eyes flickering open and shut. I walked over cautiously. "Mister Kreigman?"

"You're too late." he said, his voice full of fatigue and fear.

I looked to the bedside. There were four pill bottles there, all empty, and a glass that smelled faintly of whiskey. It seemed the demons that had haunted me and my unit since Dachau had followed Kreigman across the sea as well.

I tried to sit him up in his bed. "Kreigman! What the hell?"

"Just getting a head-start."

My blood ran cold. "Head start on what? No one is going to zombi you. Let me call an ambulance."

He laughed, a hollow, rattling sound. "No time. I'm just getting a head start on Project Verbrennung."

"What the hell is that?" I demanded, grabbing him by the lapels.

He laughed again. "Too bad, Negro. Too bad. But he will know I was loyal to the end."

"Who? Who? Is it Andaris? Tell me!"

He coughed, and laughed again, a tight, rattling sound. His eyes then rolled back in his head. I tried to shake him, even slapped him, trying to wake him up. He was gone.

I laid him back out on the bed, and looked with pity at the only Nazi whose life I'd ever tried to save.

****

"Hey, he's back. You owe me a sawbuck."

Rex fished his wallet out of his pocket and slapped a bill into Beauford's hand. "I was sure you were going to ditch out on us, spook."

I'd had about as much as I could stand, but I tried to keep it in check.

"I have a name," I growled.

"Oh, do you?" Rex asked patronizingly.

"It's Sage. Marcus Sage."

"Whatever you say, spook."

That's when I decided "team player" was out the window. I rushed Rex and slammed him against the wall, my arm across his throat. He started choking as Beauford tried to pull me off.

"Sage," I shouted. "My name is Marcus Sage. Say it!"

Beauford pulled me off, and I checked myself before I took a huge swing at him. Rex was rubbing his throat, saying, "Jesus, Sage. Just having a little fun. Can't take a joke?"

I pulled myself from Beauford's grasp and straightened my jacket. "See? You can say it."

"Yeah, he's real good with names," Beauford said. "So, now that we've got those monkeyshines out of the way, you care to come with us to talk to a contact?"

"Not Kreigman, is it?"

"We plan on paying him a visit, too."

"Don't bother. He's dead."

Beauford's eyes went wide, and he looked to Rex, who shook his head in a not-too-surprising "I didn't kill him" gesture.

"I'm sorry, did someone get to him before you could beat him to death? Don't worry. He did himself in. I went to talk to him and he'd decided a mouthful of pharmaceutical delights was better than another chat with you."

"Shit!" Rex said, still rubbing his throat. "You should've saved him."

"It was too late for that," I said, unexpectedly feeling the pang of his death deep inside me. I shook it off, and looked Beauford in the eye. "What's Project Verbrennung?"

Rex looked panicked. "Top secret, sp... Sage."

"I see."

I wheeled around and started walking back inside.

"Wait, where are you going?" Beauford asked, and the pair started walking briskly to intercept me.

I upped my pace. "Might as well go to the guy that knows all the secrets."

I managed to get into the elevator, and while Rex and Beauford called out for the operator to wait, I gave him a look that I suspected might kill a lesser man and told him to go. He shivered a little and complied. I heard Rex and Beauford shouting after me, and banging on the elevator cage-door.

I got to the sixth floor, and walked calmly past the secretaries there. Director Brody's door was closed, and I could hear him talking to someone, but I knew Rex and Beauford were on their way. This wouldn't wait.

I pushed the door open to see Brody speaking with a ghoul. She was short, maybe five foot even, and her left cheek was missing. She turned and looked at me, and I swear there was a little bit of fear in her eyes.

"Dammit, Sage, do you know what a closed door means?"

"Do you know what 'Project Verbrennung' means?"

I got a death-gaze from Brody, and the room went completely silent for a second. He then turned his attention to the ghoul.

"Pardonnez-moi, mademoiselle, mais j'ai d'autres affaires à régler. S'il vous plaît attendre dehors. Vous serez pris en charge, je le promets."

The ghoul nodded, and kept as great a distance from me as possible as she left. For a moment I wondered just what could make a ghoul so terrified.

"Where did you hear that term?" Brody asked.

"Don't worry," I said. "It wasn't from here. Whatever it is, your secret is safe. The man who mentioned it to me is dead, and he's not coming back."

"Kreigman?"

"Maybe."

"I want you to forget you ever heard that word."

I frowned. "I bet you can ask your agents to do that, but I'm not one of those yet."

"You're not going to let this go, are you?" Brody's voice

was restrained, but I could hear the anger in it. I'll admit, I almost backed off. Then I thought of Kreigman, dying in fear, and my nerve solidified.

"You know I'm not going to."

He sighed. A long moment passed as Brody made up his mind how much trouble I was worth. I like to think that, at that moment, he remembered Dachau and decided to cover my back one last time.

"All right. But this ... this is so top secret that even I could get shot for telling you. Got it?"

I nodded. He continued.

"The German Totensoldat project wasn't just about bringing the dead back to life. They knew the war was going to be over soon enough, and they wanted to be sure that the zombis couldn't be used against them. So they set a fail-safe. Every year, a certain ritual has to be performed. If it isn't, everything goes crazy."

"And now it's about to go off?"

Brody shook his head. "We've got it under control. We know the ritual."

"Kreigman said--"

"Kreigman was a delusional, drunk old man we squeezed for all the information we could. Do you seriously think he could've held out from us? We've been controlling this for years."

"Then why doesn't the public know about you defending them from this?"

Brody frowned. "Some people in this office are glory-hounds, and despite what you might think of me, I'm not one of them. We beat the Nazis, Sage. You were there. Do you think it's worth a little press to let the populace know there's a doomsday weapon out there in the heart of every zombi walking? Even with our control, do you know what sort of panic that's going to cause?"

"So you just keep secrets, then?"

"It's what we do, Marcus!" He began to get red in the face. "It's our job!"

"Your job, maybe. Not mine."

That was it. He stood from his desk and pointed to the door. His voice went from furious to icy.

"Get out, Sage. If you show your face here and haven't decided to play ball with us, I'll have Rex and Beauford escort you out. Got it?" The "escort" in his voice came with an implied side-order of a beating, or worse.

"They try to touch me, and I'll put both of them somewhere you'll need your 'ritual' to control them."

Brody glared at me as the room fell into an icy silence. That was it, then. I put my hat on, turned, and took the back stairs out of the building.

****

I'd told Marvin I'd give him some time to see whether he could remember more details of anyone who might've had power over Fred. I've never lost a sibling; I was an only cub, but I'm well aware that mourning takes time. The second time around for a loved one I can't imagine it's any easier, even for someone who's also gone through the dying process already.

There was a newsstand on the way to the Blackpoole run by an old ghoul who'd lost a cushy house and lifestyle when he'd lost his life. He was pretty bitter about the whole thing, and I tried to buy from him when I could. That evening I snagged a paper and a copy of a hard-boiled detective magazine with a lurid cover. I figured, since I still wasn't going to be allowed into the club, I'd at least bring something to read if Marvin was busy.

I turned the corner that led down the long, soot-stained block to the club, and as the distant big-band music began to pound, I caught a look at the paper and froze.

On the front page was another of those damn stories; the ones that let the higher class feel they need to be protected from the dead. This time, a ghoul woman had gone crazy in a butcher shop, stabbing a clerk and a customer with one of the shop's own knives. She'd been taken down by an officer who happened to be walking his beat nearby. The story was full of hyperbole about how terribly violent the undead were, and thanking whatever powers that be that the brave officer happened to be there.

It wasn't the terrible journalism that had me stuck, however: It was the photo. There, in black and white, next to photos of the victims, was the grainy image of the ghoul I'd seen when I barged into Brody's office.

I knew Brody was never going to tell me what this all meant, but the whole coincidence sent a shiver up my spine. I tucked the paper under my arm and walked the remaining two blocks to the Blackpoole.

Ironically, I felt as though I'd hit a dead end. What Marvin told me had pretty much eliminated most outside forces, except those who might've come to the club. Getting a list for all the people there would be impossible; not only were names generally not taken, but also the visitors from the wealthy side of town were using *noms de guerre* anyway.

I decided my best bet was to just sit and watch. The club would be open tonight. I'd have given Mamu credit for having nerves of steel to open it back up, but it was Halloween; if anyone wanted to get their undead itch scratched, it would be that night.

Marvin had agreed to signal me if anyone strange, or rather, stranger than normal, tried to come in. What exactly I was going to do from there, I was unsure; Mamu still didn't want me inside. I'll admit I was a little rankled. The BNA would only help me if I played their game. Mamu was manipulating my ability to get information on a case that she, herself, had asked me to take up. I felt hobbled.

I leaned against the wall in an alleyway nearby as I waited for the evening crowd. A couple of kids with sheets over them ran by, and I suddenly felt nostalgic for the days where the idea of the dead coming back to walk amongst the living was just something out of a spooky story.

Then it hit me. It had to connect. The girl had been talking to Brody... About what? Verbennung? Would she have burned down the shop instead of going on a stabbing spree? Was that what drove Fred? From what I'd seen of the BNA, they were more than willing to lie to those outside the organization. Maybe even about something as big as this.

I'd decided it was worth Mamu's wrath to push the issue, maybe even lie myself a little. Wouldn't be the first nor the last time I'd done so... Though I felt a little queasy doing it to Marvin and Mamu.

Marvin was at the door, solo. He looked grim; moreso than usual. As I reached the entrance, he put up a hand.

"No time, Marvin, I don't care what Mamu wants, this is life-and-death."

"As much as I appreciate that, sir," Marvin said, "she's not here. She'll be back in a couple of hours. Said she had important business. If you want to come back...?"

I wracked my brain, trying to come up with someone, anyone who might know as much about necromancy and might be able to help me. I looked to Marvin, and suddenly had a thought.

I whistled the tune of the arsonist zombi.

Marvin flinched.

"You know that tune."

"Fred whistled it from time to time."

"But it's more than that, isn't it?"

Marvin hesitated a moment, then nodded. "Before he came back, Fred never knew how to whistle at all. When he started doing it, I asked him about it and he clammed right up. Like when we first come back, he was angry, but... even more than that, you know? Any time he whistled that tune... he was in a bad way."

My heart started pounding in dread excitement. I'd caught onto something, but it was something so thin that pushing it might make it fall apart completely. Still... I didn't have a choice.

"It wasn't just that, was it?"

Marvin looked concerned, a man looking for an out. "He never whistled outside of that. We never talked about it. He didn't want to say anything. No... No it was more like he couldn't say anything. Like something held his tongue about it. But he did... He did once..."

"Did once what? This is important, Marvin!"

"We were downtown, doing errands. Near the Andaris Building."

"On Logan," I said. Pieces were falling into place.

"Yeah. He started to whistle, but this time.... I've never seen him look so terrified, even in life. I got him out of there. Got him home, he... he just wouldn't stop shaking. But after? He couldn't remember it happening. Not at all. I never brought it up again."

"The Andaris Building." I muttered, getting this horrible sinking feeling. "Look, I need Mamu to know about some things, okay?"

Marvin nodded. "I can leave her a message."

I took out some scrap paper and my pen and hastily scribbled the details of what I knew, and what I suspected, of the Verbrennung Project. "Give her this. There's a phone number to my neighbor, Barney. If she can't help me, but she has any information, have her call him. He'll find me."

"Certainly sir."

"And Marvin? Thank you. I think I'm finally going to end what killed Fred. Finally end it."

The nod was slower now, more... relieved. "Thank you, sir. Thank you."

I hailed one more cab and told the hack to take me to Logan Street. I was going back into a lion's den that I thought, hoped, and prayed I'd never have to return to. I was going to face down Tilman Andaris one more time.

****

Two ghosts passed me on my way into the Andaris Building. Kids dressed up for trick-or-treat. I shuddered as I saw them, but it gave me an idea. There was no way in hell that Andaris' security was going to let me into the building. Not after I'd made fools of them less than a week previous. In fact, I'd likely get shot for even attempting it.

Not so, however, a man in a ghost-sheet showing up for Andaris' Halloween party. I was completely covered and the guys at the door didn't even blink as I followed a wicked witch and a flying monkey in. One of them even wished me a happy Halloween.

The elevator took us to the sixth floor, where the party was going on. The entire thing was in high gear. I felt for the gun in my pocket, just to reassure myself it was there. I hated the idea that this might end with me in a shoot-out with a crowd of people. The problem was, with the costumes and masks, I had no idea where Andaris himself was. Heck, there were people even dressed up <u>as</u> Andaris.

I took out pen and paper again, and wrote a quick note on it, then walked to one of the servers and told him it was imperative that Mister Andaris receive the note immediately. I folded the paper in my last five-dollar bill and handed it over. The servant gave me a polite, curt nod, and headed into the crowd.

I headed for the roof.

Three minutes later, the door opened, and Andaris came out with a hulking zombi. He looked at my sheeted form, and scowled. "What is this all about?"

"The note not obvious enough?"

He held out the scribbled paper. "'I know about Project

Verbrennung?' You figured you'd just sign your own death warrant?"

I let the cloth slip from over me. "I just had to be sure, Andaris."

His eyes went wide, then narrowed. "Sage."

I started to take the gun out. "You're going to tell me how to stop the ritual. I know the BNA has been keeping it at bay for the longest time, but I also know those arsons are the beginning of the chaos that Verbrennung is bringing. What changed?"

"Kill him."

I don't know what I'd expected. That he'd tell me everything; confess that it was he that was bringing the end of things? I must admit, I'd hoped.

I pulled the gun, but the zombi was much, much faster than he looked. He backhanded it away from me and it sailed off into the night. I tried to duck past him, but again, too fast. He grabbed my arm and twisted hard. I felt something tear and a lightning bolt of pain shot through me. He pushed, and I dropped to the ground.

I rolled to one side, trying to get up, but my arm gave me the no-go as the zombi lifted me up by my pant leg and dangled me over the side.

"Everything all right here?"

I heard a pistol's hammer click, and I could've kissed Barney at that moment. He was standing in the entryway to the stairs, pistol in hand. Mamu had gotten in touch with him.

Thunder rolled in the distance, and suddenly... Everything went to hell.

"Nothing wrong." Tilman said, giving Barney a friendly nod, "Just taking care of some business. Seems Mister Sage figured out about Project Verbrennung."

My eyes must've been as wide as dinner plates as Barney shook his head. "That's disappointing. Still, all's well that ends well, yes? It's well-known he had an ax to grind with you. Shame that he tried to kill you here. Toss him."

I snapped out of my shock just as the words were coming out of Barney's mouth. Reaching down, I snagged onto the sheet I'd been using as a costume, and yanked quick and hard.

As fast as the zombi was, he was still an uncoordinated undead mass. He toppled backward, and I grabbed onto his coat as he did. He pitched to the side, and I sprang against him, slamming all my mass and might to push him forward. He teetered at the edge of the building. I heard Andaris call out in horror as I drew forth every bit of strength I had left and bore through the pain in my freshly broken arm to give one more almighty heave. The zombi windmilled his arms, then pitched over the side of the roof. A moment later, I heard the sickening crunch.

But I had no time to celebrate my little victory. I was up on my feet, and Barney was leveling his pistol. Andaris yelled, "You son of a bitch!" And charged directly at me.

With my broken arm, I was praying for this to happen; Andaris would spoil Barney's aim, and I could hopefully fend off the older man long enough to find my damn gun.

The gunshot ended that prayer. I dove and hid behind a chimney as another bullet ricocheted near me and Tilman Andaris, the most powerful man in Chicago, collapsed to the roof, blood pouring from his chest.

I tried to keep my head straight as another bullet clipped the side of the chimney.

"You shot your own man?"

"Oh, don't worry. Having Tilman was useful, but let's face it, after Verbrennung, none of this will be important."

I could see my gun just a few inches from my foot. I stretched out, hoping Barney wouldn't notice.

"Sage, I'm sorry, I always heard how smart you were. This obviously isn't one of those times, and you're not getting a second chance."

"Barney? What the hell?"

"Do you know how hard it was to keep on top of you all this time? Make sure you lost all your contacts? The family I had to have killed, the fires I had to set, to make sure you took the place next to mine? And all this time you were stumbling over the detritus of my work. The formulas Herr Braun... Did you know your former client was my cousin? Doesn't matter now. You never figured that out. That girlfriend of yours I had to control. Every time you came so close to knowing who I really was. Every damn time I thought you were going to crack it all wide open and foil the Reich's plans. And now you just stumble into it. Is that how you solve all your cases? Blind stupid luck?"

"It gets me by. You're a necromancer?"

"Still stupid and arrogant. I'm not a necromancer, Sage. Andaris had necromancers a'plenty. You took one off the board. I'm *the* necromancer. The gwambi. You saw me the first day you saw the dead."

He began to whistle that damn tune, and my blood turned to ice. "You were at Dachau?"

Barney laughed. "Of course I was. You yourself shot some of my men there. You have no idea how much I cringed when I found out you were working cases that brushed against my work. Each time you came a little closer, with your oafish ways. And I couldn't just kill you without drawing attention to whatever you were working on. But now that all ends."

"You're going to destroy the city?"

"Going to? It's already started, Sage. And you think too small. The entire nation will be up in flames!"

I got my foot right to the tip of the barrel, but I couldn't finagle it any closer. I cursed silently.

"Why? You lost the fight, Barney... Or whatever your name really is..."

"Typical American. We weren't fighting a war. Not my people. We were learning the secrets of life itself! Zombis and ghouls were just the first step! We were breaching heaven's walls, and we stood on the threshold of true immortality! And then you destroyed it. Destroyed everything. And you have the audacity to paint Germans as villains? As corrupt? Andaris was more corrupt than we could ever be! Our work was pure!"

"And it didn't matter how many people had to die for it."

"It did not. And now you'll be another one of them, Sage. I can see your gun now. Too bad it's out of reach."

I heard him walking toward the chimney, and I prepared to lunge for the pistol in the wild hope he'd miss if he shot at me.

"Saageee ...."

I looked around the chimney to see Barney pausing and looking behind him as well. There, Andaris was trying to sit up. Blood poured from his chest, but the stubborn old bastard refused to die.

"The ritual... is in my office..."

Barney spun and fired two more rounds into Andaris' head. It was my moment. I sprung to my feet and rushed past Barney, knocking him off balance. I then sprinted down the stairs as fast as I could.

I hit the sixth floor, and the party was still going full-swing. I was pretty sure Andaris' office was on that floor as well, and I knew I was only fooling myself if I thought a crowd would limit Barney's murderous intentions.

I plowed through the crowd as fast as I could, with pain shooting up my arm at every impact. It would only be down one more hall, near the front stairs, and hopefully I'd be able to find what Andaris had been hiding there before Barney plugged me.

Suddenly I heard screams ahead. The party-goers parted. There, at the stairs, was Andaris' bodyguard; the zombi I'd dropped off the roof. His arm was mostly torn-off, and he limped at a horrible pace, splintered bits of the femur sticking out of one leg. No one would mistake that for a costume.

He moved straight toward me, but now he wasn't so fast. I managed to slip by as his hands grazed my neck. Just beyond him was the office. I just had to keep moving.

There was a gunshot, and the hall cleared even more quickly than I thought possible. I tried to open the office door, but it was locked. I turned to face Barney, and the zombi turned to stumble toward me.

"So close and yet so far, Mister Sage. Don't worry, I'll bring you back. You can serve me just like Tilman did."

He pulled the trigger, and the pistol clicked.

I couldn't help but grin through the pain. "Didn't count your ammo, did you?"

I slammed hard against the door, causing pain to rocket up my side and stars to dance in my vision, but the lock gave way. Just beyond it, Andaris' personal office, looked like a nightmare given form. Blood-spattered walls and grizzly bits of bone were everywhere. Sickly yellow candles surrounded an altar with occult paraphernalia on it. Barney shook his head, and began to chant the necromatic words that I suspected would bring the zombi back to full power and send him to kill me. Thunder rumbled, and I almost collapsed from my pain.

Out of the corner of my eye, I saw my salvation, or so I thought: a small obsidian knife. I'd seen this very thing once before, in Mamu's hands. I had no idea what it did, but I knew it was an item of power. I'd only hoped a rank amateur like me could figure out what to do with it.

I lunged for it just as the bodyguard turned my way again. His hand was reaching for my throat as I held it up, hoping beyond hope my hunch was right.

The bodyguard's eyes clicked closed and opened. A moment passed. He turned.

I don't know how recently-uncontrolled zombis choose their target. I just know that the man who killed Andaris seemed to be at the top of his bodyguard's list.

He charged, and Barney panicked. His chant changed, but before he could get two words out, the zombi's huge hands clutched the necromancer's throat and began to squeeze. I stopped.

Barney began to flail and kick, and reached out a hand in my direction, pleading for help.

I shook my head. "This is for Fred."

After a few moments, Barney stopped kicking. His eyes rolled back, and he moved no more. I collapsed to the floor, and over the screams of the guests, I could hear the sirens approaching.

****

The police showed up due to the gunshots, and I got them to call the BNA before they got my ambulance. Rex and Beauford showed up, along with Brody. I gave them the news. They moved quickly, and, from what I later learned, covered up every damn thing they found in Andaris' offices. Tragic homicide. Jealous lover. The newspapers were full of it for weeks. Another lie on the pile.

Two days later when I got out of the hospital, I heard that there'd been a small wave of arsons, again, in the Necropolis, but that certain zombis seemed to've stopped their violence almost immediately after starting it. Andaris had been as good as his word, and the BNA had figured out whatever they needed to from what they found in the millionaire's office. The threat of Verbrennung was over. At least for the time being...

Mamu sent flowers. We were good now, and I knew it, but I also knew that there was always going to be a darkness there. I'd spend a good deal of the next few years dancing that tango with her. Sometimes the music was good, sometimes it was awful. Something kept us together throughout all of it, until the entire Necropolis paid the price back in '63.

And that's how it was. The city had been indirectly saved by the man I'd been trying to see destroyed, and in the process, he'd been killed by my friend, whom I then helped murder. Mamu was right. There were days nothing made sense. Still, the city was safe again, and I still had a business to run. A day later, I was sitting in my office, trying very hard not to think about all the things that almost happened. The rain was pouring down like it would never stop, and suddenly, there was a knock at the door. It would be the start of a case that...

...But I'm rambling. That case is the story for another day.

Acknowledgments

-To Denise Lhamon- For her excellent brainstorming and artwork.

-To Jennifer Meltzer- For fantastic editing service.

-To Dave Robison- For brainstorming and miscellaneous fabulosity.

-To Vicki, For having my back in many ways.

-To Zo and Kailey- For keeping my creativity and sanity flowing.

And now, a sneak peek at:

Case Files of the Undead

Book One

The Case of the Scarlet Starlet

****

Everyone wants to come to Hollywood. Everyone. They want to see the glamour and the movie stars. Some of them even want to be stars, so they pack their back and run off from whatever hick little burg they grew up in. They hop on a bus with the last of their money and they come here, and they expect to be discovered. A few weeks later, they're doing whatever they can just to get by.

Some people want the dream so badly, they'll die for it.

And some of those that do? They come back.

That had been the story a year or so back. A sweet young thing from some spot on the map of Kentucky who had milked cows while her brothers had gone to war had packed it up and made the journey just as the leaves were turning back home. Just as the bus had crossed into Hollywood, however, it had been hit by a truck. No survivors.

At least, that's what the tabloids said.

Any way you sliced it, Genevieve Rose walked out of her little down-home life, and became the first ghoul to light up the silver screen.

Oh, sure, there had been creepy little films made by creepy little directors in creepy little towns, but Hollywood never did anything small. Despite the risk they were taking, Ozmark Studios put that pale, beautiful, homespun flower in their new picture, 'I, Renfield.' Cornel Wilde and Gregory Peck fought a duel over her on the sound-stage created ruins of her farm. The kiss at the end of the second act was almost enough to shut the whole thing down under the Hayes code, and after Cornel admitted he hadn't minded the kiss at all, and suggested he might've flubbed a take just to get another shot at young Genevieve's lips, well... There was more scandal over one film than Hollywood had ever seen, and believe me, if you don't know the town, that was saying something.

Of course, Hollywood ate it up with a spoon.

I'd not seen the picture when that fatal Friday rolled around. The week had largely been a wash: I got stiffed for a divorce bill, a complication I'd seen coming a mile off. I'd been called off of a missing ring case when it was found behind a couch, and the work I'd done in the Boone brothers' poisonings had gone exactly nowhere.

That morning, the world had stubbornly refused to end. I suspected the rest of the divinations of my fortune cookies the night before would be equally untrue, so I settled into my office not awaiting a marriage proposal or good fortune.

The door remained sadly unknocked for the entire morning. I'd done the crosswords. I'd fed the fish. I'd stared at the calendar until I swore it was staring back at me. At that point, I was desperate for anything to break the monotony, and considered closing up shop early to hit the local theater. The picture they were running wasn't really any good, but the popcorn was fresh, and the air conditioning was nice. I heard they might've been running a Zorro short before the film, too...

But the daydreaming had delayed me to the point that fortune did, in fact, intersect my path. That day, fortune's herald was a silhouette outside the smoked glass. Tallish-looking woman, handbag. I'll admit, it was only partially the fact that I was desperate for distraction that I called out "Come in." before she knocked. The other half? If I got to it first, I always looked considerably more like a magician than I actually am.

The door opened, and I suddenly wondered if perhaps I'd just dreamed the entire day. It would've explained the weird fortune cookies. But I didn't have dreams as odd as the situation was about to become, so I simply nodded and tried to keep my jaw from dropping.

At five foot nine, Genevieve Rose looked pale yet strong on the screen. Now, within my office, she was stunning. I won't hesitate to say that. She was beautiful, and I realized that, despite what the gossip rags might say, mister Wilde had very good taste.

She stopped just inside, looked at me quizzically, then... Blushed. I was doubly amazed. It was something most ghouls couldn't do. Somehow, she pulled it off.

"I ... Take it you know who I am?"

I stood and motioned for her to take a seat, "I think anyone who doesn't obviously hasn't lived in this city very long. Please sit, miss Rose."

"Thank you." She sat, and I could now see the little tell-tale greyness in her features. Still, it did nothing to mar her, and my heart beat just a little faster.

"Now, how can I help you?"

She gave a little smile, "No small-talk. That's nice."

"Sorry, I get businesslike when there's actually business."

She smiled a little more, "I've gotten used to studio types. Either deferential to a fault, or wanting to drone on and on about minutiae."

"I take it that doesn't sit well with you?"

She shrugged a little, "I get tired of it. But I won't foil your laconic opening."

"My what with my which now?" It was my turn to hide a blush.

"Your short way with words, mister Mix."

"Ah," I said, sitting back on my side of the desk, "Yes. That. So..."

I let the moment hang. She actually looked for a moment as if she wasn't going to take the conversational bait. She was toying with me... But she didn't give me time to decide if I liked it.

"I want to hire you, mister Mix. I understand you're an excellent investigator."

"I like to pride myself on that, yes. My fee is twenty dollars a day, with a-"

She reached into her purse and took out a roll of bills big enough to choke a sizable dog. It made a pleasing little thunk as she dropped it on my desk, "All yours if you can pull this off. Quarter of it if you can't."

I blinked. "All right. What's the job?"

She looked me in the eyes, and for a moment, I almost felt lost in them. Her voice went cold as she spoke.

"Quite simple, mister Mix. I want you to find out who murdered me."

I paused, and took a drink, "You're joking."

"Why would I joke about my own murder?"

"Well, first of all, most people know how they died."

"But not all."

I nodded to that, still playing along, "There are two other reasons. One, you weren't murdered. You were killed in a bus accident."

"It's what the press would want you to believe."

"Your press?"

She frowned. It was a hit and she felt it. She reached to the shoulder of her dress, then turned her back to me. Gently, she pulled it down in one of the most up-close stripteases I've ever been witness to, much less one that happened in my office.

Down just below her now-bare shoulder blade were three holes, each the size of a dime. The skin had been artfully recovered around them, but...

"Shot in the heart. From behind. Does that convince you?"

I nodded, shaking my mind from the fact of seeing that lovely pale skin back to the case at hand; and make no doubt about it, it was a case now.

"I agree. That's a murder."

Genevieve covered her shoulder again, quickly, as she turned to me. She looked...Relieved, as if she might've told this story before.

"I'll write you up a contract."

"What was the third?"

I paused as I was taking the carbon paper out of a desk drawer.

"Third?"

"What was the third reason you thought it was a joke?"

It was my turn to frown. "Before I was a dick, I worked for the Los Angeles Police department. Every once in a while, we'd get some actor or actress who just wanted to ride along with us and play 'cop', to better portray it on the screen. No offense, but your type can be a pain in the ass."

"None taken. I've worked with enough of 'my type' to know."

I started writing up the contract. "Figured it might be another like that."

She shook her head and signed on the dotted line, "I hope I'm not too much of a pain for you, mister Mix."

"Shan't think you would be." I said. I'll admit, I left my eyes on her just a second too long; she smiled. She knew who held the cards here. I'd folded like an amateur.

"Where can I get a hold of you?" I asked, realizing too late that I'd just given her a tighter leash around my neck.

To her credit, she was merciful. "Here," She fished a business card out of her clutch and placed it on my desk, "I only give this to my favorites. You can get in with it. Please stop by tomorrow, tell me what progress you've made. All right?"

She turned to leave as I picked up the card. It had 'Willshire Springs' printed on it in raised, precise script.

"This is quite the swank place. May have to get a new suit."

I looked up, and she was already gone. For a moment I wondered if I'd dreamed the whole thing, but the card and the thick roll of bills were evidence.

I'll tell you, though, there are days I wish it had all been a dream.

About the author

James Silverstein was born and grew up just outside of Chicago and has been writing fiction since the age of 9, the day he was given his first typewriter. (and 'Dragonman', the draconic superhero was born!)

He has been involved in theater from the same age, including some professional Shakespeare in the 90's and has recently played his dream role; Bottom in Midsummer Night's Dream.

James has written for various role playing games, including 7th Sea, Stargate, and, most recently, Cairn. He is currently working with Dave Robison and Ed Greenwood on a spate of novels, audio dramas, and gaming projects over at Onder Librum, and one day hopes to both inspire other creative-types to bring out awesomeness.

Also, he hopes to become the sole monarch of Mercury!

Made in the USA
Lexington, KY
08 December 2016